SINISTER SAILING

A MIA WATSON CRUISE SHIP MYSTERY

GWEN TAYLOR

JEN BOOKER

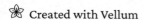 Created with Vellum

Gwen
For my dad, who loved a good mystery, whether it was the riddle of the Sphinx or reruns of Columbo.

Jen
To my husband, my partner in crime who supports me in whatever I do and takes me around the world on real-life adventures and my parents for instilling in me a lifelong love of reading

CHAPTER
ONE

The boarding ramp groaned with passengers heading onto the Bella Blanca cruise ship for a long weekend to the Caribbean.

And I, Mia Watson, was finally one of them.

Luck had been on my side this year. When a four-day holiday weekend at Labor Day had aligned with the murder mystery cruise package from Miami to Haiti, I simply couldn't turn it down. I'd one-clicked so fast, my head and my wallet had spun for hours after. It had taken a nice chunk of my royalties and a lot of convincing my husband Shane, but it was going to be so worth it when we won the game and the prize of a two-week, all-inclusive cruise aboard the Bella.

I wanted that prize so bad I could taste it.

The winner would get to choose when they traveled, and I just knew two weeks of fun and sun would be the vacation I'd been needing, the restart my writing was begging me to take. Everything would improve. If only I could win it...

We took a few steps forward, and I could now see the purple welcome banner hanging on one of the upper decks that said "Bon voyage, Sleuths!"

Excitement skidded down my spine. I wanted this trip to be an experience neither of us would forget. An anniversary to remember, especially since lately we'd been ships passing in the night, no pun intended.

The ship's horn sounded, signaling embarkation was almost complete. It wouldn't be long before the anchor was raised, and we'd set sail.

I looped my arm through my husband's, forcing him to put down his phone. "Can you believe we're actually doing this?" I couldn't. I was finally here after years of dreaming of the Bella's famous whodunit weekends.

Shane answered me with a grunt and a weak pat of my hand. He didn't want to be here, but I could work on him.

I scanned the crowd, trying to guess which of

the passengers would be joining in the Murder Mystery Weekend I had been counting down on my calendar like it was Christmas.

I spotted a man in a tweed cape and matching double billed hat. Check. Definitely my people. His enthusiasm made me feel better about the squeal I felt bubbling just below the surface.

I wanted so badly to turn to Shane and say that the game was afoot, but not only would he not appreciate the reference, he'd probably bolt back to shore where he'd been complaining he wanted to stay since I'd booked this anniversary vacation. I'd always wanted to join a murder mystery event, but Shane never could see the point of trying to solve a fake murder.

So, instead, I flashed my brightest smile at him and tried to make my excitement contagious. "I wonder when it will start. The itinerary they sent doesn't say." I dug around in my beach bag and produced the paper I'd printed. "But dinner is at eight, so maybe it starts after that? I'd like to freshen up and look around first, wouldn't you? Give us a head start."

Shane barely seemed to register my words. He craned his neck in every direction.

"What are you looking for? Girls in bikinis?" I

teased.

His head whipped around. Now I had his attention.

"What? I can't look around?"

"Lighten up, honey, it's a vacation. I can't even remember the last time we went away together. And it's our anniversary! Try to have fun. Please," I added and sent up a silent prayer that the trip would go well. I loved my husband, but he wasn't always fun to be with. Once he decided he wasn't going to enjoy something, he never came around. We were bordering on that now. Especially since we were waiting in the Florida heat.

The line started moving faster, and we found ourselves gathered into a group in front of an official-looking man in bright whites and a very pretty woman in a short tennis skirt.

I nudged Shane. "It's like The Love Boat. Ready for romance?"

I could have sworn he blushed, but he gave me a tight-lipped smile and reached for the papers being passed around.

"Here's your schedule," Shane said.

"Don't you mean 'our schedule'?" My eyebrow raise was lost on him because he was looking around again. "Are you sure you aren't being tailed?"

I couldn't help the quip. I knew I shouldn't antagonize him, considering his current mood, but he really was acting as though he was expecting to see something or someone. Or maybe I'd just been watching too many murder mysteries in preparation for the weekend and thought everything was a clue.

I chose to shake it off. We were about to have a great weekend doing something I wanted for once, and I wasn't about to lose my good mood.

I decided I was even going to make small talk with the other participants milling about, something my usually introverted self would never do at home. But, we weren't at home. We were on vacation, and I could be anyone I wanted for the next few days.

One lady in particular seemed to want to keep talking to me, even though I wasn't as lively as some of the other people who were obviously here for the mystery event. Like the guy wearing the deerstalker hat. And some lady dressed in a frumpy outfit with a giant knitting bag and jaunty little sun hat. She'd come as Mrs. Marple, I was sure of it. So was the lady chatting happily to me about murder.

"Lookit, Mrs. Marple came prepared, didn't

she?" My chatty new companion gestured toward the lady who'd struck up a conversation with a lean man in a cassock. "I should have worn a costume."

I laughed and gave her a wink. "You look marvelous as you are. No worries."

And she did. She could have been a well-preserved seventy or a hard-lived fifty. It was hard to tell, but she was decked out in a brightly patterned coordinated top and bottom set with white wedges and a giant hat covering a stylishly-cut head of cherry red hair, save for a single thick lock of white tucked behind one ear. She also had on enough jewelry to start a mall kiosk and a sense of style that put her right at home on a sailing ship. Something told me she had a great sense of humor, as well.

Looking at her, I self-consciously pulled the rubber band out of my own auburn hair, which was thankfully still free of any unwanted wisdom high-lights as I entered my forties. I felt a little frumpy, but unloosing my hair might not have been the best idea. The wind was whipping it around, and it needed controlling. But that ugly, hair-pulling rubber band I'd salvaged from the car's cup holder was all I had on me.

I smoothed my tunic over my leggings and

wished I had spent a little money on some cruise clothes. I hoped I wouldn't feel too out of place.

The colorful woman tipped her giant hat at me after the conversation over our fellow sleuths lulled. "Perfect weather, isn't it, dear?"

She fished around in her giant tote, pulled out a large bottle, and spritzed herself generously with a sunflower-scented perfume.

I was prepared for it to choke me into an asthma attack, but it was more subtle and really quite nice compared to the aroma that had begun to swell from the crowd battling the heat of Labor Day and close quarters on a gangway. Shane's aftershave was starting to expand in the heat. Not that I didn't love it, I did. It had been his signature scent since I'd known him, but lately, he'd been a little too generous with it to the point that I worried about his sense of smell. Our bathroom was heavy with cologne in the mornings now, like I imagined Old Spice headquarters might be in a heatwave.

"It really is great weather." I brought myself back to the moment. "We couldn't have asked for better."

The weather *was* perfect, and I was excited to be here. Maybe I should talk to her some more. If Shane wanted to be a grump, I could leave him to it and talk to someone who was here to have a good time.

CHAPTER
TWO

There was no time to brood over Shane's mood as we were herded into a large room filled with tables for four. A server showed the three of us to one of the low tables and informed us tea would be served shortly.

I took in his formal uniform, down to the white gloves. My first high tea! My first high tea on my first cruise on my first murder mystery weekend. I wondered what other firsts might be in store for me.

I realized we'd only exchanged pleasantries with our new acquaintance, not names. So, I extended my hand and introduced myself. "I'm Mia, by the way. Mia Watson."

"Edith, Edith Eddington. My friends call me

9

Edie, and you can, too." She paused and struck a pose. "Edie, like Sedgwick."

I must have looked nonplussed because she explained Edie Sedgwick had been Andy Warhol's muse. The reference was a little before my time, but I told her I saw the resemblance.

Shane's phone buzzed. He read the message, and his already sour expression took a turn for the worse. I smiled at Edie. "That's my husband, Shane." I whispered conspiratorially, "This isn't really his thing, but he's very accommodating." I reached over to stroke his arm, but he shifted away in his seat.

Edie's smile dimmed a bit, but was quickly reenergized as a tall, sandy-haired young man with a lanky frame and an absent-minded professor look came up behind her with a big smile for her and an extended hand for me. "Hi, I'm Kevin."

"My grandson," she explained, introducing us formally.

I made a second round of introductions to Shane, but didn't make any more jokes about him. Not that I thought he would mind. He was sending texts as fast as he could type and whoever he was texting with was keeping up the same pace. With each incoming buzz, his scowl deepened.

I turned my attention to our tablemates as Kevin pulled out a very expensive camera. "Hope you don't mind being on camera, we're kind of vlogging our trips."

Trips, plural. Interesting. Wonder what the unusual pair was up to?

"That sounds...fun." My introvert soul cringed at the idea, but I could see Edie loving the spotlight.

I started to ask about their trips, but another white-gloved server arrived with a trolley laden with delights. He lifted a tray so we could have a closer look.

I selected two finger sandwiches: salmon and cream cheese and cucumber. I wasn't at all sure I would enjoy a cucumber sandwich, but I had read about them in so many books, I couldn't miss this chance.

As we nibbled on our tiny snacks, a second server arrived with a variety of teas and coffee. Edie and I had tea with milk to go with our cucumber sandwiches. Kevin had a black coffee. When Shane asked for a beer, the server was momentarily thrown off but quickly made a beeline for another server heading out with an empty trolley.

Edie and Kevin told me all about their travel vlogging plans in between more servers offering us more sandwiches and just when I thought I couldn't eat another bite, the dessert trolleys appeared.

As I eyed the bite-sized delicacies, I found my second stomach. "I'll have one of each." To his credit, the server kept a blank face. Shane on the other hand, let out a small grunt. I ignored him and hoped Edie and Kevin hadn't heard.

They were happy to follow my lead, and each had the full assortment of desserts. Kevin, bless him, went for two of each. Each of the small sweets was only two or three bites, I reasoned. Plus, we were on vacation, and everyone knows vacation calories don't count.

I was just about ready for a little food coma when the captain whistled for our attention. That woke me up! The servers immediately disappeared, taking their trolleys with them.

I took in a few deep breaths. The murder mystery could begin at any time, and I didn't want to miss a thing.

I was disappointed when it became clear the captain merely wanted to herd us from afternoon tea to the safety briefing.

"Would everyone please follow me for the muster drill!" He repeated himself several times over the chattering crowd. Finally, he gave up and began walking in the correct direction, shouting 'muster drill.'

I pulled Shane along like a fussy toddler but paused at the sound of raised voices. The other passengers were filing into the room, and Shane was suddenly eager to get to another beer. I wanted to keep listening to the fight I was pretty sure was going down.

It was hard to understand all the words over the crowd of murder mystery participants, but I definitely heard a man and a woman arguing at the railing. Sure enough, when we got closer to the ballroom, there were two ship employees having it out.

The woman pushed against the man's chest and stalked off. She saw me, and her demeanor changed in an instant. She was suddenly all smiles, but I knew that was for my benefit.

I was shocked when, a few short minutes later, she joined the captain at the podium inside the ballroom.

The mic wasn't on, so I couldn't hear a word, but her posture indicated that theirs, at least, was not an adversarial conversation.

I leaned over and nudged my husband. "Look! It's her."

Shane bristled. "Her who?" He was looking behind us and not at the woman we'd just seen shoving her coworker.

"Her, at the podium. She's the woman we saw fighting with that dude like a minute ago."

"I didn't see anything."

"They were arguing. Literally just a minute ago. How could you have missed that?"

Shane rolled his eyes. "I must have been minding my own business. Why do you always have to be so nosy?"

"It's called attention to detail, not being nosy. I'm a writer. It's my job, really, if you think about it."

"It's your hobby."

I blinked, suddenly not seeing clearly. Since I'd taken 'a break' from writing, Shane hadn't stopped putting in little barbs about my lack of income. Thankfully, royalties still rolled in, just nothing like I'd been getting. And he wasn't letting me forget it. Which made my anxiety about not writing even worse.

I needed a new proposal for my editor like yesterday, but for some reason, I had nothing in the tank.

It'd been six months since I'd written a single word. Sometimes, I would feel a flicker of inspiration, but by the time I sat down at my computer, it was gone.

It seemed that my sense of romance was dead.

But my attention to detail was not. Plus, I was good at multitasking, so I let my eyes roam the room, searching for clues.

Behind us, I noticed a striking woman walking alone. There was something familiar about her, but I couldn't put my finger on it.

I felt bad for her, all alone. I told Shane we should invite her over, but he nipped that in the bud with another of his barbs.

"Keep your nose out of it. She probably doesn't want to be bothered." He glanced around the space and lit up when he saw the bar over by the back exit. "I'm going to get a drink."

"I think this debriefing is required for every...one..."

The words died on my lips. He'd already disappeared through the crowd.

"Mia! Mia, over here!"

I looked up to see Edie and Kevin had snaked through the crowd and were waving at me to join them at one of the tables.

Shane wasn't going to ruin it for me. I knew from experience I couldn't turn his mood around, but I needed this chance to recharge and get my groove back. I could sit alone and abandoned, or I could meet new people and enjoy myself. I chose the latter.

"Hey again. Thanks for letting me sit with you guys."

Edie patted my hand. "You're very welcome. Isn't this exciting?"

"Yes, yes, it is very exciting." I shook off the bad mood Shane had brought on and focused on the safety briefing. I listened closely in case a clue was worked in to the usual spiel, but I couldn't help wondering about the fight I had just witnessed. Besides, other than saying 'don't sue us,' the drill seemed to be very basic information, like fire safety and how to wear a life jacket.

Edie and Kevin were hanging on her every word, unlike me. I shook my head. I needed to focus again. Maybe if I missed something, they'd clue me in, so to speak.

I'd no sooner vowed to pay attention to the presentation when I saw the man who'd been shoved earlier slide in behind the captain at his table just as the woman finished her speech.

"Edie, have you been listening? Who is she?"

"That's Angela, and Johnny Come Lately there is

the cruise director, or I miss my mark. I guess the boss can turn up when he wants," she snarked.

The captain, a white-haired man that reminded me of Leslie Nielsen, stepped up to the podium to say his final words, but my gaze was on Angela white-knuckling the mic and shooting daggers out of her eyes toward the man she'd pushed as he took his seat behind the captain.

She didn't make a move to budge from the podium, so the captain stood beside her and took the mic.

Captain Belmont, we learned, loved murder mysteries. After a joke about a killer whale that didn't quite make the splash he intended, he began the debriefing by thanking the woman still standing there like a statue. "Let's give our Assistant Cruise Director, Angela Anderson, a round of applause. While Angela passes out your dossiers, I would like to take a moment to introduce someone else you should know, our Cruise Director, Lucas Chalmers."

The word 'dossiers' cut through the chatter and suddenly, you could hear a pin drop.

The room was silent except for the introductory remarks from Cruise Director Lucas, but I barely registered that he was speaking. I was entirely focused on our girl Angela as she made her way through the crowd, handing out the large packets with her expensive manicure and perfectly coiffed hair.

I thanked her when she handed me mine and quickly pulled out the contents out of my envelope in record time: a double-sided sheet of paper with a story and the rules of the game, a small notebook, and a pen.

The paper had QR codes in several places, giving participants the option of getting a hint in exchange for a time penalty if they got stuck. Cheaters. I wouldn't be getting any hints, I told myself.

I turned my attention to Lucas in time for him to place the mic back on the podium. Oops. I had let my attention wander too long.

There was a smattering of applause, but it seemed I was far from the only distracted member of the audience.

Lucas didn't seem to notice. He gave the group a wide smile as Angela returned to the podium with empty arms. She reached for the mic just as a loud noise behind us had the room of weekend sleuths gasping and turning toward the jarring cacophony.

Something that sounded like falling cymbals had our attention just before the whole room went completely, disorientingly dark.

CHAPTER

THREE

There is always chaos in darkness.

And this was no different. People were moving in all directions, bumping into each other, and generally freaking out. With noted exceptions, of course.

The three of us were calmly holding firm, as were Mrs. Marple and the other two costumed gentlemen she'd seemed to band together with. We supersleuths stood together in a small cluster listening for clues like the pros we all probably thought we were.

Edie took out a flashlight from her enormous beach bag and shined it around the room. Kevin did much the same, but used his cellphone.

I thought that was a good idea and was in the

process of reaching for mine when a second loud noise came from an adjacent room.

I made my way toward the spot I remembered the light switch being. At last, I found the wall and followed it around until I felt the switch and flicked the lights back on.

Dim orange light flooded the ballroom. I blinked at Edie's flashlight hitting my eyes at the same time.

"Sorry." She clicked it off and dropped it back in her ginormous bag. To the crowd, she yelled, "Nobody move."

But it took her putting her bejeweled fingers in her mouth to make the world's loudest whistle for the group to turn its collective eyes toward her and Kevin.

"That's more like it. We need to stay put." She looked around the room, like she was counting heads, and I did the same.

The room was literally chaos. Everyone had moved, trampling the bags or tripping over them, and a number of dossiers had been dropped. Several people seemed to have left the ballroom in the confusion.

Suddenly, the doors at the main entrance to the ballroom swung open and a handsome man burst through pushing a catering trolley in our direction.

An elegant white tablecloth was draped across the otherwise empty trolley.

I took in the gold-accented hem just inches from the floor and wondered, as I had at the afternoon tea, how he kept the front edge from catching in the wheels. When he reached our group, he paused and looked around.

"I'm looking for Lucas," he announced. When no one answered, he added, "The cruise director. He should be here."

I nodded and told him Lucas and several other people had slipped away while the lights were out.

He thanked me and pushed the trolley into a back room. Through the open doors, it looked like a storage area for the ballroom. I could see tables and chairs stacked in the back and music stands lined up in front.

The door closed behind him before I could see more. Not that I hadn't tried. Maybe Shane was right, I was nosy. I considered that for a fraction of a second. No, not nosy, naturally curious, observant, I decided.

I barely had time to congratulate myself for my healthy curiosity when a wail rang out from the storage room. "Noooo! I need help!"

I locked eyes with Edie and Kevin. As one, the

three of us raced toward the sound. I wasn't sure, but it's quite possible Edie used her large bag as a shield to push through the throng of bystanders just, well, standing by.

I didn't need an engraved invitation. I pushed the storage room door open and looked around. Out of sight through the ballroom door, near the side-wall of the storage area, was a man lying in a pool of dark red.

Kneeling over him was the trolley man who had been searching for Lucas. He turned the body until I saw the face. It would seem he had found our missing director.

The man put two fingers to Lucas' neck and looked up at us with a grim expression. "He's dead."

CHAPTER FOUR

I glanced around in disbelief. Why had this man tracked through the blood with the trolley? His shoes and clothes were covered in red as though he had crawled through the mess on his knees.

Edie nudged me. "Doesn't he watch TV? You only destroy evidence if you are guilty. Then again, his being the killer would be too easy."

The rest of the group had pushed their way in, crowding the available space. Some of the more aggressive men were jockeying for position to have a look at Lucas. Edie and I were getting pushed a little too close to the pool of blood, fake or not, for my comfort. And there was a slightly unpleasant scent of onion that must have been coming from the trolley post lunch. I did not want to be pushed any closer.

Kevin did his best to keep them from crowding in any closer, spreading his arms like a human barricade.

I immediately started taking mental notes, and I saw Edie had her phone out, pecking at the screen furiously.

Someone in the group yelled to get security which caused Kevin to wink at me. I let a small smile escape before making my face as passive as possible. No use letting others get ahead by realizing what was happening.

The trolley man caught our exchange and wriggled his eyebrows at me before addressing the group.

He cleared his throat and raised his hands as if to quieten the crowd. "No need for that. But we must find the killer before he or she strikes again."

I grinned at the understanding that rippled through some of the slower uptakers.

The trolley man gave me one final eyebrow wriggle and went back into character without a hitch. "He's dead! There's a killer onboard the Bella Blanca!"

I locked eyes with Edie and Kevin. It was go-time, and we were ready.

They pored over their handout. Mine was already crumpled within an inch of its life from my eager and slightly sweaty hands. I had most of it memorized, and besides, I could revisit it after I picked up some clues.

I wondered where Shane had gone, but there was no time to lose figuring this thing out. I wanted to win.

First things first, I pulled out my phone and took pictures of the scene as I scanned the rest of the room for clues. The thing I most feared was over-looking something that was in plain sight. I scoured every inch of the room and it paid off. I noticed a bloody handprint on the far wall by a side door and went to examine it. That had not been there before. Had it? Surely not.

Near the handprint stood an empty plinth. I went towards it to inspect it and knew immediately from the scent of sunflowers that Edie had joined me.

Without turning, I asked, "Doesn't this look like something should be sitting on it?" I was studying the plinth for any hint of what should have been there from the scrape across the dust and the shape left behind.

"This is a storage room. Maybe it's a spare," Edie pointed out.

True. Or a bluff for the sake of a group of murder mystery weekend sleuths.

Time was wasting.

I decided to take charge. "We need to take a good look around before all of the clues are destroyed by these people." I watched the spectacle of the crowd trampling through the pool of blood and touching the bloody handprint. "Kevin, why don't you take that corner?"

"Sure thing. What should I be looking for?" He asked.

"Anything that looks out of place. Or bloody."

He gave me two finger guns. "Find blood. Got it." He edged his way through the group to the door.

"Edie, do you think you can get into that side room without anyone noticing?" I kept my voice low.

Edie followed my gaze and grinned. "Is a cat proud of its bumhole?"

Having had several cats in my lifetime, I agreed that, yes, it was, and watched as she effortlessly melted into the crowd and disappeared from view.

I gave the room a good once-over again, scanning it for anything that stood out and noticing the competition sleuthing over the room.

The crowd had separated into small groups. Any evidence on the floor had been obliterated. I could barely even see where the trolley had rolled through the 'blood.'

I needed to talk to the man who discovered the body first. That interview could prove crucial to solving the case. After all, he was our opening act. And that trolley had my attention.

I watched the man heave the trolley into motion. It stuck. He looked like he worked out. A trolley shouldn't take that much effort to set into motion. With some effort, he got the cart moving, forcing weekend sleuths to make a path as they headed for the door. He seemed to not hear a thing now, because he wasn't stopping for any questions.

The crowd swirled behind him, immediately refilling the gap. I followed him and the trail of disturbed evidence out onto the deck of the ship as quickly as I could in the chaos, but by the time I exited the ballroom, he was gone. I thought I saw faint lines of pinkish-red headed for the cafeteria. That made sense. The trolley was a catering item. Maybe I'd need to talk to the whole waitstaff.

I made my way to the galley through the bustling cafeteria where passengers here for the long haul and not just the weekend were having their very generous repast.

I spotted Shane among them, at the counter with a mimosa in hand, blending right in with the sauced patrons. His nose had gone tellingly red, so I knew he'd managed to down at least a few rounds of drinks already.

"Hey stranger!" I took the swivel stool beside him and leaned in for a sip of his drink. "Could have used you in there. What did you see? Did you leave before the lights went out?"

Shane was eyeballing me with a bored look I knew too well. He sighed and gave in to my questions. "No, I left right after that. You were off with your new friends. You didn't need me." His voice had become petulant, as though I had been ignoring him and not the other way around.

I bristled, but he was right. I didn't need him. After all, maybe it was better than having to constantly pull him into it. He was going to find his way to the bar no matter what. I puffed at my bangs that had fallen over my right eye and fixed my "fine" look on my face. "I'll meet you for dinner, then."

I scooted off the stool and headed toward the galley. The swinging double doors were unattended. I leaned in close and heard the normal bustling sounds of food being prepared.

I hoped I was in the right place. I took a deep breath and pushed through.

Getting my bearings took a minute. Food for the buffets was being prepared, and no one looked out of place. It was a bustle and flurry of movement that left no opening for me to chat anyone up. I made my way toward one server, only to have them walk away and leave me standing there before I could utter a single word. I sighed.

I was bungling this and, worse, I'd come in here and failed to find the main guy I needed to see. There was absolutely no sign of the trolley man.

Maybe I was wrong. Maybe the trail didn't lead here. Maybe it had been a false clue.

I was ready to give up and push back into the dining area when I saw the red-stained coat of a waitstaff uniform hanging on the back of a stainless steel fridge.

Bingo.

I wove in and out of the ballet familiar to restaurant staff everywhere, dodging servers and cooks until I made it to the line of refrigerators and a door off to the right of them marked Private.

I glanced back. No one had taken notice of me.

Please be unlocked, please be unlocked.

I tentatively turned the doorknob.

No dice. *Fudge.*

"What are you doing here?"

I turned around so fast I was sure I'd given myself whiplash.

The man standing in front of me was glaring at me with unconcealed menace.

"Who dares to enter my galley?"

"Me, Mia. Me, I'm Mia, I mean. Part of the mystery group. I followed a clue--"

"Follow this." He pointed his knife at the exit. "Good day."

I swallowed hard. Looks like I'd gone out of bounds. "Sorry. I didn't know."

He made no attempt to let me off the hook. Instead, he kept silently scowling with his arm still frozen in a get-the-heck-out gesture that I meekly followed.

I had just wasted a good ten minutes. Dadgumit.

I left by the glowing exit sign the chef had pointed to and came face to face with Edie and Kevin.

An explanation started tumbling out of my mouth. "I saw a blood trail, but--"

Edie didn't let me finish my sad tale of failure.

"Later." She grabbed my wrist. "Come with me. You aren't going to believe this!"

CHAPTER
FIVE

E die pulled out her dossier and her notebook. "I've cracked the case!" she crowed. "Or found the first red herring."

She admitted that last part with a self-deprecating shrug, but with a wry smile that said she knew she was at least onto something. Edith Eddington was no one's fool.

"I made it into the side room without being tailed," she began, lapping up the limelight. "Someone had left a note with a puzzle on it. I do cryptic crosswords every day, so it was a snap to solve."

Her grandson motioned for her to hurry up. "What did it say?" Kevin was even more impatient than I was.

"I'm getting to that!" Edie dramatically flipped to the first page of her notebook. "The message said, 'The truth will set you free.' Too easy! There was a number scrawled there, like maybe money. It said 10K. I went to the information desk. Saw the lady on duty." Edie gave a coy shrug. "She had information alright."

"And? What did you learn from her?" I was losing my patience, too.

"Gossip. Lucas was in the middle of a very messy divorce! Very messy!" Edie cackled, then realizing how loud her voice had gotten, snapped her mouth shut and looked around for anyone who might have overheard her.

There was a man in his early sixties lurking nearby who looked like an angry high school coach, complete with a purple and gold ball cap and beige track pants straining to contain his gut. I hoped he hadn't heard, but his self-satisfied grin told me he had been eavesdropping.

I grimaced. He was going to be trouble, I just knew it. But we were obviously more clever than he was, because we didn't need to steal clues.

"Did you learn anything concrete about the messy divorce?" Now that Coach was gone, we needed to get back to work.

"Well, it would seem that our handsome Mr. Lucas was a bit of a playboy. A man with a girl in every port, or rather, starboard and aft." She wriggled her eyebrows. "Handsome devil. Back in my day, I'd have been an aft girl, too."

She cackled again and Kevin smiled, not embarrassed at all by his grandma's joke.

"Ooh, an affair. Those always end badly," I said.

Edie nodded. "His problem is. . . *was*. . . that his wife works on board, too. I guess he wasn't as good at juggling women as he thought he was. You think someone wanted him to pay them off? With that 10K scrawled on there?"

Kevin whistled. "Wow, wife and mistress on the same boat. It takes some brass, um, you know what I mean, to try something like that. And someone was bound to find out, of course. But, wow, the bal-brass."

I couldn't tell if he was impressed or disgusted. Maybe he was a bit of both. What kind of man would cheat on his wife right in front of her face? The ship wasn't big enough to hide something like that. Or maybe it was. What did I know? One thing was for sure, however. His wife was better off without him. Speaking of which, we needed to interview her. After all, if murder mystery shows had taught me anything, it was that the spouse is always suspecto numero uno.

Edie started listing all the forms Lucas's cheating had taken. Phone calls and texts that had him leaving the room, after-hours meetings that turned into working dinners, and when he was around, he was always tired. Sounded like most of the relationships I knew.

I looked at Kevin. "Who did you talk to? Did you learn anything?"

"I thought I was supposed to look for blood?"

"Okay, did you find any?"

"There was lots of blood. I don't think there was anything useful, though. Too many people walked through it. According to the dossier, there are three more employees close to Lucas that we need to find. The clue they included is that we should find people that, quote 'you can relax around.' What do you think that means?"

"Well," I considered, "you can relax with a spa treatment. Maybe one of the employees that has information is a masseuse."

"Right. So, I need to find the places to relax on board? Won't that be most places? It is a cruise."

"True, but I have faith you can find the right three people 'you can relax around.' Edie, you and I need to find that trolley and examine it, then grill the grieving widow and the side tart, see what shakes out. I think these are our best suspects. Agreed?"

Edie and Kevin nodded, affirming in unison, "Agreed."

"Good. Alright, team, let's go catch ourselves a killer."

CHAPTER
SIX

Edie and I went off in search of the man who'd pushed his trolley through the pool of blood when he found Lucas on the floor. We needed to talk to him. He should know where to find Lucas' widow and girlfriend.

I stopped a passing cruise employee, a small woman with black hair neatly pulled into a tight bun and described the guy. "I'm looking for a man who is tall, dark, and handsome. His hair is cut short and just starting to get a little silver at the temples. He has big, brown eyes."

Edie laughed. "Were you taking notes purely for the murder mystery, or was that extra credit?"

I pretended to ignore her, but I felt my cheeks flush. Who wouldn't notice him? He was H-O-T hot.

"Do you know an employee who matches that description? Maybe in culinary? He was pushing a trolley and looking for Lucas earlier."

The employee shivered a little, but recovered quickly, except for the grin she couldn't wipe off her face. "I think you're talking about our security off-I mean, one of our caterers, Brady. He should be near the pool, serving lunch to the captain today." She pointed and quickly continued on her way.

"I don't think she should quit her day job," Edie whispered in a not-so-subtle aside. "Do you think we were the first murder mystery players she's spoken to?"

"She did look rather excited, or anxious, to answer the question." I agreed, keeping my voice lower. "Was that her natural response, or were we supposed to get something from her?"

Edie shrugged. "I don't know. I'll make a note." She opened her notes app and pecked away. "There, just in case. Now, let's head to the pool and chat up this handsome trolley man."

We picked up our pace and were at the pool in no time. Sure enough, there was Brady, still in his role as a server, despite being outed by his fellow crew member as a security officer. He was being grilled by the guy I could only think of as Coach, and the gang of cosplayers led by Miss Marple was already heading away from the pool area. Anxiety about being late to the game hit me in the gut. I needed this. Badly.

We'd just have to speed up our investigation. It was our turn to sneak up and listen carefully.

Too bad Coach was trying to Bad Cop the information out of Brady, and the tall, dark, and handsome trolley man wasn't having it. Coach may as well have been talking to a stone. But he did let Coach inspect his trolley. He even lifted up the tablecloth for him.

"Charming your way to a win?" I asked by way of greeting.

Coach glared at me. "He doesn't know anything useful." With that, he turned on his heel and stalked off toward the stairs.

"With his looks and personality, he must have to beat the ladies off with a stick," I said to no one in particular.

Beside me, Edie craned her neck to watch Coach stalk his way toward the cafeteria. "Oh, I don't know. He has a little something something. Wouldn't count him completely out."

I half-expected her to say she'd hit that, but she

only turned on her own charm, which was real and captivating, and pointed it full force at Brady.

"But he's got nothing on you, sugar."

Brady smiled. "You're too kind, ma'am. How can I help you two lovely ladies?"

I was momentarily distracted by his smile. It lit up his eyes, and having it directed at me with what seemed like appreciation was momentarily disorienting. If Shane still smiled at me like that, maybe I wouldn't be distracted at all.

I sighed. I looked at Brady and cut to the chase. "We don't have a lot of time. I want to go over your trolley and ask you some questions."

He shrugged and lifted up the tablecloth for us to inspect. "Have at it."

Our search yielded nothing. The trolley was clean. It must have been a red herring. I took a few photos, just in case.

Dang it. I cleared my throat. "Okay, nothing there, but we were hoping you could tell us how to find Lucas' widow and his on-board girlfriend."

Brady seemed genuinely surprised. "You two aren't just pretty faces, are you? If you've gotten that far this fast, you may beat the record for fastest crime solvers."

"Not if you don't answer our questions we

won't." Edie had her notes app at the ready. "Lay it on me, sugar. You can sweet talk us later, over drinks."

Brady laughed. "It's a date. Now, who do you want me to talk about first? I can't just spill my guts the first time you bat your eyes at me."

"Less flirting, you two, more facts." I tapped my notebook. "I guess we should start with the widow. Is there anything you can tell us about her?" I looked up into his big brown eyes and batted my own dramatically for effect.

He let out a hearty laugh and gave me another smile that warmed me down to my toes. "Well, since you asked so nicely, I suppose I could tell you a little gossip I heard." He paused and carefully emphasized, "This is only gossip...but...a few months ago, there was a rumor going around that his wife, Violet, had gotten tired of his philandering, but she wasn't tired of his family's money."

He paused to see if we'd taken all that in, then nodded. "Now, I can add what I've seen myself. She's been causing trouble for him at work. If I had to guess, I would say that she's been pushing him to give her a divorce on her terms."

I frowned. "Okay, but what about him? Did he want to get a divorce?"

Brady winked. "You do ask good questions. Actually, I don't think he did, but his girlfriend might have wanted him to. And he has the kind of lawyers that don't play around, if you know what I mean. His mother would have seen to it that his wife barely left with the shirt on her back. In fact, I heard he wanted to take her assets as well, including her cherished family summer home. And with his lawyer, he'd have done it, too."

Cherished? That had to be in the murder mystery script, but it was a great clue. We had motive.

I thanked Brady and asked him where we could find Violet. He flashed his dazzling smile again. "I think you'll find her in the bar at this time of day. You should talk to her. As I said, I've only repeated gossip. You never know what to believe." He winked and walked away.

I shuffled Edie towards the bar and reviewed our clues.

"She's the killer, I just know it," Edie said, taking out her phone to text Kevin. "She'd have lost everything, even if the divorce was her idea. It sounds like Lucas was a vindictive man—cheating on her then trying to take her family property when she wanted out. Now she doesn't have to lose a thing, and she's got insurance money to boot."

Kevin intercepted us on the way to the bar. His face told us his news before he even opened his mouth. "Hey, I got nothing. You?" He shoved a hand through his windswept hair.

Edie gloated. "We've got a hot tip! Join us on our pilgrimage to the bar."

That perked him up, but I could tell he was disappointed he wasn't the one with the news to share.

But when we got to the bar, Violet wasn't there. The bartender was happy to chat, though.

"I haven't seen her all day," the bartender said before offering us drinks. Being on a mission, we declined.

"On second thought, I'll have a Shirley Temple." Edie smiled flirtatiously. As the bartender poured the mocktail, she casually asked, "Does Violet come in here often, uh, Sam?" Edie asked, squinting to read his nametag.

Bartender Sam placed the drink on the bar in front of Edie. "She likes a sundowner. And some-times, a *lot* of the time, she likes some company."

My ears perked up. "What kind of company?"

Sam smirked. "Let's just say she doesn't like to

be lonely. She has lots of friends to keep her company."

Okay. That was interesting. I guess they both played games.

"Do you remember the last time you saw her?"

He put on what I called a 'thinking face' and looked into the middle distance. After a moment, he finally had a reply. "She was in a few nights ago."

Kevin let out a loud sigh. "Was she alone?" He sounded as impatient as I felt. I wanted to grab the man's lapel and shout, 'Tell me what you know, Bucko!' but I was hiding it better than Kevin.

Kevin's tone must have gotten through to the bartender because he came through at last.

"She was with a friend. A man. The two of them are in here once or twice a week."

We all three spoke in unison. "And?"

The bartender recoiled from us like we'd struck him. "Uh, they had some champagne."

I exchanged glances with Kevin and Edie. We needed more than that.

"Were they celebrating something?" I prodded, wanting to add, 'Like planning her husband's murder?' But I kept silent, waiting.

"Umm, I think they were talking about her family's summer home. She got pretty wound up about it. Then," he looked around, like he was about to divulge something he shouldn't, "you didn't hear it from me, but I heard Violet say she wished Lucas would fall overboard."

We digested that for a moment.

"Oh, and, get this," Sam lowered his voice even further.

We all leaned in to hear.

He was playing this up for all it was worth.

He pushed the towel over the shiny surface of the bar and pretended to be cleaning before adding, "Rusty, her friend, he said he could make it happen."

Edie was scribbling in her notebook. I was pretty sure I could remember 'wife planned to have Lucas thrown overboard.'

Kevin rolled his eyes. "Imagine that. Okay, I think we got it. Grandma? Ms. Watson? Ready to find this Rusty guy?" He looked at Bartender Sam. "What does he look like? Do you know how we can find him?"

Sam must have reached the end of his script because he clammed up. "Sorry, folks, but I'm afraid I've said too much already."

Kevin huffed and showed us his phone. "We've only got another half an hour tonight."

That focused our minds. We hopped up and

thanked Sam. Edie threw her Shirley Temple back, downing it in one, and handed her glass to him with a wink.

"No time for flirting, Grandma. We've got to find this Black Widow."

"I'd never! Go on, Kev, lead the way!" Edie slung her oversized purse over her shoulder and trotted after Kevin with me following behind, only a few seconds off their heels. I could have sworn I'd seen Shane on the dance floor, but when I stopped for a second look, I only saw strangers in the dim light. The sea air must have addled my mind. I couldn't even get Shane to dance at our wedding reception.

But maybe he would be willing after dinner. After all, fifteen years should merit at least one dance.

I hurried after Kevin and Edie. We only had thirty minutes of scheduled sleuthing left. Dinner and dancing would have to wait.

CHAPTER
SEVEN

I caught up to my crime solving partners.

Kevin's gaze swept to me as he continued his questions with Edie, ending with, "Who else can we 'relax around?'"

"Don't you think we should look for Violet? We can interview the other employees tomorrow." I looked at my watch. "We've got twenty-seven minutes."

Edie craned her neck. "Where is that nice young lady with the bun?"

"The Concierge Desk should know how we can find Violet, if she's an employee," I suggested as I pulled out my map of the ship.

I pointed it out on the map and looked around. It

wasn't very helpful if we didn't know where we were starting from.

Kevin pointed to the bar. "Here we are. Let's go."

Edie and I did our best to keep up with his long strides, but he left us in his dust.

I puffed, decidedly not fit enough for all this trekking around. "I guess we'll meet him there." I tugged Edie's arm and pointed toward the elevator. "Let's go this way."

We caught a break. A ping sounded only a few seconds after I pushed the button.

But then the door opened, and Coach greeted us with a grunt as he moved over to let us in. "Hurry it up. You two are slowing me down."

I rolled my eyes and selected our floor. "On your way to eavesdrop on some other sleuths?"

Coach glared at me. "Hmph. I don't need no help."

"We could trade information, you know," Edie said with a suggestive grin she cast out like a fishing lure. If I had to guess, it wasn't just information she wanted to trade with him.

He gave her a wry side-eye with a smile turning up his grumpy lips. But he was still silent. The floors were ticking over. We were almost there. *Come on...*

Finally, his shoulders sagged. I could literally see

him giving in to Edie's siren call. Hook, line, and sinker.

He offered her a flirty grin. "I may have heard some stuff."

I willed him to hurry up. "Go on." We had—I checked my watch—twenty-six minutes left to find clues tonight.

The elevator dinged, and Coach gestured toward the opening doors. "Ladies first."

We exited, and he looked at us expectantly. "So, what've you got?"

"Oh, no," I reminded him, "you already got some of our information. This was your turn."

His eyes narrowed. I thought he might walk away, but after a moment, he offered a little nugget of information. "Angela, the chick with the dossiers..." he looked at us to see if we could remember as far back as that.

"Yes, we remember her." My voice was sharper than it needed to be, but time was short, and so was my patience.

He didn't seem to register it, or care if he did. He continued, "Angela was up for the cruise director's job, but Lucas, the dead guy, got promoted over her."

That was interesting. A scorned wife, a bitter

coworker, and a girlfriend we still had to find out about. The trifecta. Maybe all the women in Lucas' life wanted him dead.

Edie patted Coach and pretended to fix his collar as she tucked our old paper clue from earlier into his shirt pocket. "Here's our first clue for your trouble. And while it's been great talking to you, sweetie, we've got to go. I'll see you later if you're having dinner in the lounge, at say eight. I'll be in a red dress." She didn't wait for his reply. She simply grabbed my hand and led me in the direction of the concierge.

The words 'not fair' punctuated with a swear came from behind us.

Edie shot me a wicked grin and yelled back over her shoulder. "I can't keep my grandson waiting! Be sure to wear your dancing shoes!"

We hustled away as fast as she could manage. Once we were out of earshot, she giggled. "He owed us one, anyway! I'll make it up to him at dinner."

"If he shows!" I laughed, impressed by Edie's confidence.

Edie didn't seem perturbed. "Oh, he'll show alright. Trust me."

Kevin was waiting at the Concierge Desk. "What took you so long? We're almost out of time!"

"We knew you could handle this on your own. We had our own avenues of inquiry to pursue." Edie informed him. She pulled out her notebook. "Now, where can we find Violet?"

Kevin's shoulders slumped. "He, uh, the concierge, said we need to take this golden opportunity to relax. Same old, same old."

I could hear the defeat in his voice.

"Well, we've got a little more time tonight. They seem stuck on the relaxing bit. So, where should we go to relax?" I asked, not willing to give up just yet. Hmm. "Where is 'a golden opportunity' to relax is the question, isn't it?"

Just then, a bell rang out and lights started flashing. My eyes bugged out. "A casino!"

We rushed toward the clanging sound.

CHAPTER
EIGHT

K evin and I practically carried Edie as we
hustled down to the casino at the other
end of the corridor. The flashing lights
and bells and whistles cut off before we got there,
thank goodness.

There were a handful of passengers trying their
luck at the tables and slots, including a raucous
game of poker in the back corner. A quick glance
around, and it was obvious who the big winner
was—an elderly woman sitting on a customized
mobility scooter tricked out with colorful banners
on six-foot high flag poles and a hot pink basket in
the front.

We had only been on board a few hours, but a
few of the slot machine jockeys looked as though

they had already blown their gambling budget. The looks they were giving the old woman could drop an elephant. I wondered if she would have to floor her scooter to get out of there.

I had never seen the thrill of one-armed bandits, but we all have our vices and expensive hobbies. To each his own. I imagined Shane thought the money we'd spent on this trip had been flushed away just as efficiently as the chips the gamblers were losing to the house.

Kevin and Edie dragged me back to the present and our mission. Edie pointed out a croupier standing alone at her roulette table.

"Let's see if she can help us 'relax.'" She paused and turned to Kevin, who had a slack-jawed look on his face. "Don't you get any ideas! We're solving a murder. You can find a pretty girl to help you relax on your own time!"

I wasn't sure if the cackle that punctuated her words was because she amused herself, or because her words got a blush out of Kevin.

Ignoring her, I made a beeline for the lonely croupier, a strikingly beautiful young brunette whose name tag identified her as Svetlana. I dug out my room card. "Excuse me, could I use my room card to get some chips, please?"

"Of course. How much would you like?" She took my card, and I did some quick mental math.

"Um, fifty dollars?" I didn't have to spend it all, right? I could cash in any chips left over when we got what we needed.

She returned a moment later. To her credit, she didn't bat an eye as she handed over the miniscule stack of plastic tokens along with my key card. She had exchanged the generic cruise line sleeve for one advertising the casino. I shoved it in my pocket and made a quick wish that the fifty bucks would soon be credited back to my account.

The croupier included us all in her next question. "Would you like to try your luck at roulette? I can explain the rules if you've never played before."

"Who, me? I don't gamble." As she spoke, Edie plucked the top chip from my hand and placed it firmly on the red diamond.

The croupier looked at me for confirmation, since it was my chip. I nodded, and she asked if there were any more bets. Then she asked us to step back, then spun the wheel.

"Red twelve. You won!" She handed me two chips. I'd just doubled my bet! Maybe gambling wasn't so bad. I wanted to have another go.

I handed a chip over to Edie. "Can you pick another winner?"

She gave me an exaggerated wink. "I've got a system!" She placed the chip on the black diamond.

The croupier again asked if there were any more bets.

My tiny win hadn't set off any bells or flashing lights, but a couple of people abandoned their black jack table and joined us. I groaned inwardly. Would the croupier answer our questions if we had a crowd? Were these people even gamblers or were they a couple of clue leeches, like Coach?

We only had a few minutes left. I was just going to have to go for it.

I cleared my throat by way of easing into my queries. "By any chance, do you happen to know a ship employee named Violet? We, uh, have a mutual friend, and I would love to catch up with her this weekend."

She gave me a knowing smile. "I know Violet. Red thirty-six. I'm sorry, you haven't won this round. Would you like to place another bet?"

Edie had plunked another chip on the red diamond before the words were out of the girl's mouth. I think I had the hang of Edie's roulette betting system.

The croupier seemed to have figured things out herself because she didn't bother to ask for more bets before giving the wheel a spin.

She pursed her lips. "Mutual friends with Violet, huh? I'm intrigued."

"How so?" I was genuinely puzzled. Who's to say I didn't have mutual friends with Violet in pretend world?

"She's more of a high roller. So are most of her friends." She gave me a pointed head to toe up-and-down. "Black two. Another round?"

Before Edie could put another of my chips on the black diamond, I took a chance and placed all of my remaining chips on black fifteen. "My husband and I are celebrating our fifteenth wedding anniversary," I explained to Edie and Kevin.

Svetlana spun the wheel. "Where's your husband? Or are you celebrating your anniversary without him?"

That struck a little too close to home. Thankfully, Kevin jumped in. "We were hoping to have dinner with Violet tonight. We're kind of in a rush."

"Well, Violet is the kind of girl who likes bad boys who stay one step ahead of the law. She might find herself with some bad boys onshore tomorrow."

She winked at Kevin, "But not all girls like bad boys."

Kevin blushed, and Edie elbowed me in the side. "It wouldn't be gambling to bet where this is headed."

I laughed, and then almost choked as the croupier announced, "Black fifteen. The lady is a winner!"

This time, I did get the flashing lights and clanging bells.

"What? I won?"

Edie pumped my hand like she expected my winnings to flood from my armpit. "You did! You won!"

"Me?" I was still processing. "For real real?"

Svetlana laughed. "Yes, real winnings. You can cash them in any time."

"Thank you! Thank you!"

I practically did a schoolgirl jump with an equally excited Edie. I was a winner! I'd never so much as gotten a dollar on a scratch-off before. I'd always only had bad luck, if any luck at all.

I took in the chips piling up in my column.

Maybe my luck was finally changing.

CHAPTER
NINE

A bell clanged right as the three of us exited the casino. But this was no winner's bell. Instead, it was the PA system. The signal was followed by Angela giving a brief announcement to the murder mystery participants that the day's excitement was over. It was time to enjoy our downtime until seven a.m. tomorrow when sleuthing could resume.

I didn't want to stop. And judging by the fallen faces of my murder-solving buddies, they didn't either. But we did have to eat and rest, and I did have an anniversary to celebrate.

Assuming I could find my husband.

"I feel too jazzed up to quit now!" Edie wailed.

Kevin tugged on her giant purse as though

reminding her to calm down and started saying his goodbyes. "Me too, but we can meet on deck, near the gangway in the morning at six-forty-five sharp. Sound good?"

Edie grudgingly nodded, perking up when I reminded her that she had a date with a red dress and an athletic supporter, er, coach.

I thanked Edie and Kevin and told them I also had a hot date--with my husband. I hoped I was telling the truth.

We headed off together in the direction of our cabins, but were soon parted. Edie and Kevin were staying on an upper deck. Shane and I were in a budget cabin down below. I pushed down a jealous pang as I wondered if the pair had a balcony. I had so wanted a balcony, but Shane had poo-pooed that idea. I sighed. It didn't matter. Cabins were just for sleeping, after all.

I pushed open the door, eager to share news of my win with Shane. But that news would have to wait, apparently, because the room was empty. I took in the wrinkled sheets in disarray and the spicy scent of our cabin. Shane must have only just gotten up from a nap. We couldn't have missed each other by more than a few minutes.

Disappointed, but still on a little high from my

GWEN TAYLOR & JEN BOOKER

big winnings, I got ready for dinner and decided to do a little window shopping in some of the shops while I waited for him to respond to my texts.

But first I wanted to go over the pics I had taken of the crime scene. We'd been too busy to look again, even if it was fresh in our minds. Maybe we'd missed something.

I studied the pics on my phone, blowing them up, sifting through them. Nothing popped, but maybe I needed a bigger screen. I opened my bag and stared at my laptop. I used to be practically glued to it, spending countless hours writing love stories. I had started earning a pretty good living, too.

Then, the stories stopped keeping me awake at night. It had been at least six months since I had written a single word. Heck, it had probably been three months since I had opened my laptop and pressed the power button. My stories were gone, and I didn't know if I was ever going to get them back.

I stared at the computer and sighed. Maybe my phone screen would be good enough. I put my computer back in my bag, unopened for another day.

I took one more look at the photos. The scene was just as I remembered it. Hectic. I decided to go over them again with Edie and Kevin. Maybe one of them could spot something I'd missed. Hopefully, Kevin had put his fancy camera to good use. Besides, I needed to get ready for dinner.

It didn't take long for me to get into my best Edith-Eddington-inspired outfit, going as glam as I could on what I'd packed. I stepped out into the corridor knowing I looked good.

My plans to head straight for the main dining room were derailed as I got off the elevator. The sun hung low in the sky. I hurried out on deck to watch the sunset. I looked around, surprised no one else had the same idea. Perhaps there was a crowd on the top deck enjoying a sundowner.

I leaned against the railing and took in the cloudless sky and the calm waters reflecting the sun for what seemed like miles to the horizon. This was a view I could get used to. I made up my mind to be on deck at this time each night. This trip may only be a long weekend, but I could make every moment count.

The gentle lapping of the waves against the boat and the slowly sinking sun were lulling me into a meditative state. I had to be careful, or I might fall asleep where I stood. I straightened up and began to stretch when I sensed someone behind me. A gentle aroma of teakwood tickled my nose.

"Fancy meeting you here, detective."

I spun around as Brady tipped his hat and treated me to a friendly smile that had his eyes crinkling charmingly.

"Although, I don't think I've ever seen a detective who cleaned up as well as you."

He was one to talk. I bit my tongue before I asked if his surname was Bond. If I had thought he was distractingly handsome in his uniform, that was because I hadn't seen him dressed for dinner. I was surprised to feel doubly glad I'd opted for glam.

I found my voice and returned his smile. "Thank you, I think." I cheekily took the opportunity to ask him a question about the murder, only to be rebuffed.

"Nope. You're off the clock, Marple. Catch me tomorrow for all things macabre. Tonight we dance." He offered me his white-suited elbow.

I checked my silent phone. Nothing. I gave in and tucked my hand in his elbow. "My name's Mia."

I turned back for one final look as the sun sank below the horizon. Brady followed my gaze. "One of the perks of the job. The sunsets never get old. Now, how about that dance?"

"Okay, but just one."

He wriggled his eyebrows just as he'd done this morning. "One is all I need."

CHAPTER
TEN

By the time my dinner arrived, Shane had finally slid into the dining room, somewhat the worse for wear. I hoped he wouldn't cause a scene. He didn't have an inside voice after he had a few drinks.

"You ordered without me? Am I supposed to watch you eat now?"

"Lower your voice. You never replied to my messages, and it's past nine." I checked my phone. "Actually, it's ten. I waited nearly two hours before I ordered. Where have you been?"

Brady chose that moment to come up to our table. "Good choice on the chicken. Porterhouse is a bit heavy for this time of night." He eyed Shane like he'd only that moment realized he was sitting there. "Well, hello. Who are you?"

"Who am I?" Shane's voice rose even louder. "I bloody well should ask you that."

I cut in. "He's part of the murder mystery crew, Shane. Brady, Shane, my husband. Shane, Brady. He might be a murderer."

Brady looked surprised, but quickly put on a poker face. "Chief Security Officer Brady Sanchez. Caterer for the weekend, and I'm no murderer, but your wife is a real femme fatale. She sure can dance. All eyes were on her." Brady bowed toward me and then pointedly spoke to Shane. "And you look like a man who has danced his fair share tonight."

Shane seemed to want to surge to his feet, but he paled and squirmed in his chair at the other man's larger form, the lines of his biceps showing through his well-tailored suit jacket. I almost felt sorry for Shane, but he'd practically stood me up and I was still irritated.

Brady tipped an imaginary hat to Shane, and to me, he said, "I'll see you tomorrow, Mia."

Shane snarled, and Brady gave him a look I couldn't read.

What had just happened? I wasn't sure, but it

seemed to take the fight out of Shane. His food was served, and he picked at it in silence.

In a perfect world, I would have been having a delightful dinner conversation with my darling husband, but since my darling husband had been in a mood the entire day, I would settle for silence.

As much as I wanted to go over the interviews and clues and examine the brief story we had been given, I didn't want to press my luck. I did have one topic of conversation that might put him in a better mood.

"You'll never guess what happened!"

He looked at me, boredom oozing from every pore. "I'm tired. I don't want to play games. Just tell me."

I paused, hurt, then did as he told me because my excitement overrode the slight. "I won over fifteen hundred dollars in the casino while I was gathering clues!"

Shane sat right up at that news. "You left all that cash in our cabin? Are you nuts?"

I sat back, stunned. He wasn't even happy for me. "No. I haven't collected the money yet. It'll be credited to our account."

I could see the wheels turning, but he didn't say anything else. He reached out and grabbed a passing server, nearly pushing her into a tattooed man at the next table. "Get me some ketchup, would you?"

"Certainly, sir. I'll be right back." If the young woman was upset at being manhandled and ordered around, she hid it well. The passenger at the next table, on the other hand, flexed, making a snake on his exposed bicep dance. Shane missed the peacocking, because he hadn't bothered to look up when he addressed the server.

The other passenger gave Shane one last dirty look before turning back to his dining companion, a pretty blond woman in her mid-thirties. She didn't look like a natural beauty, but she could have stepped from the pages of a magazine, like a real housewife with a full glam squad on retainer. In a different age, the pair could have been a mafioso and his moll.

I turned back to my plate. My dinner was getting cold, but I dug in to the bed of couscous with the fresh veggies that Brady had recommended.

It was still delicious, even if I wasn't all that hungry now. I pushed the rest of my food around the plate, feeling just a little sorry for myself.

The server returned, pushing one of those trolleys. Hers stuck just like Brady's had. I guess it made for a good red herring, but something about it was still tickling the back of my mind. I needed to review the crime scene with fresh eyes.

The girl pulled up to our table with a trolley of calorie-rich goodies and served Shane a ramekin of ketchup. "Here you are, sir. Enjoy your meal."

She turned her attention to me. "Brady thought you might enjoy this." She deftly placed a decadent-looking slice of cake in front of me. It had six thin layers of cake separated by thick layers of dark chocolate. Looking at it made me feel the need to go to confession.

I thanked her and, sensible chicken and vegetables forgotten, I tucked into the plate of sin in front of me. It tasted even better than it looked, if that was possible.

Shane shoveled his food down like a starving man and was still chewing when he pushed back from the table. "I need some fresh air."

I made a decision. "Fine. I'll meet you back in our room."

I watched him lumber off and surveyed the dining room for any sign of my new friends. Then I spotted a showstopping red dress and heard a tinkling laugh. Edie!

As an introvert, I rarely inserted myself into other people's lives, but tonight I didn't want to go back to my own life just yet. And it wasn't like Edie was alone with the cantankerous coach. She was with Kevin, Coach, and Brady, who must have caught Edie's eye because he was telling her the same thing he'd told me earlier. No sleuthing tonight.

So I wasn't the only one who couldn't put the case away when the bell rang.

I tiptoed like I was intruding, then caught myself. Throwing my shoulders back, I walked over a bit less hesitantly, although I was still thinking about turning back the entire time. Fake it till you make it, right?

I might have turned tail and run before they'd noticed I was headed over, but Brady spotted me and jumped up and pulled out an empty chair like he had been waiting for me all night.

"Mia!" More than one voice said my name, but for the moment, I really liked hearing it from Brady's lips. What was I thinking? I was here with my husband on our anniversary trip, even if he was being a pill.

"Hi, mind if I join you?"

"We were hoping you would," Edie said, throwing her bangled arm around my waist and pulling me down to sit between her and Brady.

"Brown Eyes here doesn't want to talk murder, but that doesn't mean the rest of us can't."

Coach seemed eager enough to compare notes. No surprise there. He even had Edie's crumpled note about the 10k lying by his plate.

Kevin shook his head. "You are too much. We've got an onshore excursion tomorrow, and we haven't planned anything."

Edie and I looked at him, shocked.

Edie blinked at him. "Didn't you hear--"

I put my hand on Edie's arm to stop her, before she could let Coach in on what the croupier had told us.

"Don't you remember? We talked about it earlier. In the casino." I tried to telepathically remind Kevin, or at least, I made bug eyes in his direction. Fortunately, he got the message.

Edie distracted Coach by asking him to dance, and that left the table with just me and Kevin and Brady.

"So, Kevin," I sent an apologetic look to Brady, who rolled his eyes like he knew what I was going to say, "have you been back over the crime scene photos you took? I was looking at mine--"

"Oh, yeah." Kevin took a long drink before he put

down his glass and pulled out his camera. "I got loads, lots of angles. Let's look them over."

"You two do that. I'm walking away and I don't hear a thing."

Kevin saluted him and I waved. Then we got down to business.

I opened the photo album on my phone and immediately had second thoughts about sharing with Kevin. His photos really did look like professional crime scene shots, complete with better lighting. Side by side, mine looked like a child had taken them with a toy camera. "How did you do that?"

He grinned. "It's a good camera. Spent all my college graduation money on it and this trip with Grandma. Worth every penny."

"I bet it is. Priceless. Okay, let's see 'em."

Kevin scrolled through them until we got to the body pics. Something odd caught my eye. "Is that something in the blood there? Zoom in."

I wasn't sure, but it looked like a small diamond.

The closer in Kevin zoomed the image, the more it pixelated, so I couldn't be sure.

He perked up. "Want to go over all these again?"

I did. But that was for tomorrow. "First thing in the morning. When we're fresher."

He looked a little disappointed, but Edie and Coach returned with Brady trailing after them, and the good conversation and champagne made me glad I'd put it off til tomorrow. All work and no play, after all, would make me dull. And I needed to be sharp to win this, to stir up my life. Tomorrow would take care of itself.

Tonight, I wanted one more dance before I turned into a pumpkin at midnight. Besides, I had to go back to my cabin and whatever was in store for me there. Kevin and Brady both were happy to oblige. Even Coach offered to spin me around, but Edie told him he was all hers. At least for the night.

I had to grudgingly admit that Edie had seen a diamond in the rough. Coach cleaned up well. Of course, most men do look nicer in a tailored suit than stretchy coach pants worn a bit too tight.

Looking between my two options, I took the lesser risk, accepting Kevin's offer even though I wanted Brown Eyes to be that last dance.

As I took a final spin, I let myself simply enjoy the moment. Tomorrow, as Scarlet had so eloquently noted long ago, was indeed another day.

CHAPTER
ELEVEN

Six-thirty came fast and hard, with a headache and barking dogs where my dance feet had been. I didn't wear heels often anymore, and my feet weren't used to the pain they caused.

I forced myself out of bed, quietly, so I wouldn't wake Shane. I wasn't sure what time he had come in. I had been asleep.

Despite my best efforts, the slight creak of the wardrobe door woke Shane as efficiently as an alarm clock. *If only he woke that easily for work.*

He rose up slightly on one elbow and glare-squinted at me. "Can't you keep it down?"

"Good morning and happy anniversary to you, too!" I took off my penguin pajamas as I spoke–

Shane would have to wait for the sexy lingerie I packed. I knew I was being passive aggressive, so I stopped myself. "This is our anniversary trip, Shane, and you've done nothing but ditch me and complain. I'm not asking you to join me today, frankly, because I don't want your bad attitude to ruin my fun. But I expect you to be well-rested and ready to spend some time together when I get back."

Shane opened his mouth and then closed it again. He mumbled something and rolled over to face the wall. I was disappointed, but I didn't have time to coddle him this morning.

After a quick shower, I hurried to dress and comb through my wet hair, feeling like I was late, even though we couldn't disembark until seven. But Edie, Kevin, and I needed to go over all we knew and all we didn't know.

When I made it to our agreed-upon spot, I immediately felt frumpy, and not for the first time on this trip. Maybe I should invest some of my casino winnings in a new wardrobe when I got home.

Kevin was wearing what I thought of as frat fashion—a button-down shirt, untucked, and salmon-colored chino shorts. He also had his massive camera hanging around his neck. He and

Edie were ready to document the day in ultra high definition, by the looks of things.

Edie was decked out in a flowing white blouse and colorful sarong over her bathing suit– ready for any kind of action, and all I had to set my jeans and T-shirt outfit apart was the necklace I'd bought myself for our anniversary. It was a brilliantly polished ammonite shell shaped into an elephant, my favorite animal.

"Ooh, elephants, they never forget. Unlike me," Edie said, reapplying a beautiful coral lip stain to her already perfect look. "You kids ready to crack this thing wide open?"

"I don't know if I'm a kid, but I've got my game face on. Kevin, how are you this morning? Did you stay out late?"

"Did he hook up with that pretty croupier, do you mean?" Edie asked.

"No. To both of you." Kevin's look told me it was not the first time his grandmother had asked him such a question. "I went to bed at the same time as you. Alone, unlike someone else."

Now it was Edie's turn to blush.

"What?! Did you hook up with Coach?" I don't know why I was so surprised, but I was a bit scandalized.

"Oh, hush! No such thing. We just canoodled a little. I got a few hours of sleep. That's all I need these days, anyway."

I mouthed the word 'canoodled' to Kevin, who just shrugged. I shrugged too and turned the conversation to our excursion.

"I've been thinking about what the croupier told us all night. I think I know where we need to go. Here." I dug into my purse. "The croupier must have slipped a note in when she switched my key card sleeve. It fell out when I got back to my cabin after dinner." I gave them an apologetic look. "Look, it's a business card for a beach bar, The Rum Runner. Remember what she said? 'Violet likes bad boys who stay one step ahead of the law.' Rum runners have to stay one step ahead of the law."

"And that's not all." I flipped the card over. "There was also a hand-drawn sketch of a coiled snake on the back. Look."

I pulled out the card to show them. "And when we were at dinner last night, I noticed a man sitting at the table next to us with a snake tattoo on his arm."

Edie's eyes widened. "Did you get a good look at him? Do you think it's the same guy the bartender told us about?"

"I'm not sure. He never turned his face in my direction, and the lighting in the dining room is made for romance. But I remember his tattoo. We should start our search at the bar."

Kevin nodded in agreement. "It's a good place to start. We'll have to ask around, see if anyone knows anything about this guy."

As we made our way off the ship and into the port, I couldn't help but feel a sense of excitement tinged with fear.

This was the moment we had been waiting for, the chance to uncover the truth about Lucas' murder and whether Violet hired a hitman, offed him herself, or what. I had to remember that Brady could be a suspect or an accomplice. He found the body, after all, and no one else was around.

The morning trek was mostly an increasingly hot blur as we made a few stops at local market stalls and tried to figure out just where to find the bar. By the time we got the correct route down, Edie had a few new purchases under her belt and I had a new appreciation for moisture-wicking unmentionables.

Finally, Kevin saw the sign and we all hurried toward it. I was eager to find out our next clue, eager to get to our delayed destination. But as we walked towards the beach bar, I couldn't shake the feeling that we were being watched.

The bar was a simple, open-air structure with a thatched roof and wooden stools. A few locals were casually sipping drinks, and a group of tourists were playing a game of beach volleyball nearby.

We slipped into some empty stools and ordered drinks, trying to act nonchalant. I scanned the crowd for anyone with a snake tattoo but came up empty.

Edie didn't want to play the long game. She went straight for the bartender, reeling him in with flattery and charm. It was a masterclass in people-wrangling. One I could definitely learn from.

After a few minutes of small talk with the bartender, I couldn't resist casting out my own line and asking about the man with the snake tattoo.

The bartender's face darkened, and he leaned in close to me.

"I don't know who you're talking about," he said in a low voice. "But if I did know anything about him, I'd tell you that you're better off leaving this place and never coming back."

Despite the heat, goosebumps prickled my arms. Something about the bartender's warning seemed genuine and urgent. They sure made these games seem real.

"We're just here on vacation," Kevin spoke up, trying to defuse the tension. "We're not looking for any trouble."

The bartender looked at us skeptically, then turned his attention to another group of patrons. We finished our drinks quickly and left the bar, feeling more confused and lost than ever.

As we walked back towards the ship, Edie grabbed my arm.

"Hold on a minute. Something's not right. We need to find out more about that man with the snake tattoo. If the bartender is warning us to stay away, it means we might be getting closer to something. Isn't that how this usually works?"

"I agree," Kevin chimed in, pulling out his phone and starting a new video. He panned the camera toward us and motioned for us to talk. "Ahem. If you two want to win this thing, we need to keep pushing forward. Don't forget, he's playing a part. We can't let these warnings--" Kevin stopped abruptly. He grabbed us each by the arm and pulled us into a shadow. "Is that him?"

He was looking at me, pointing out a man a

short distance away. He quickly opened up the camera at his neck and aimed it at our mystery man.

Edie craned her head around him. "Which one? They all have tattoos."

Kevin pulled her back into the shadows, keeping his camera aimed so it looked like he was filming us, but the suspect was in the background, an unwitting photobomber.

She smacked him away, almost knocking the very expensive camera from his hand. "He's on the move! We've got to tail him!"

We did our best to blend in with the tourists, checking out the souvenirs in front of each shop, but never let him out of our sight. It wasn't difficult. He stopped again and again to look at T-shirts and keychains and whatever souvenirs were on display. Either he was actually a tourist, or he was also trying to blend in.

Kevin filmed Edie talking about the trip, but I was sure he was filming the tattooed stranger over her shoulder.

Twenty minutes and several cuts in Kevin's vlog later, our patience was rewarded. The man sat down at a cafe table occupied by two women wearing bikinis with tiny sarongs and oversized sunglasses.

Two very familiar looking women. Snake

Tattoo's dining companion was having drinks with another woman I was sure I had seen in the ballroom when the captain welcomed us all on board.

This had to be the right guy! Now we needed to get close enough to eavesdrop.

The couple at the next table started packing their things, so I swooped in to claim the chairs as soon as they were vacated. We took over the table with as little noise or fuss as possible. Even Edie seemed to realize it was time to use her inside voice.

The man was speaking quite gruffly, but the wind was picking up, and it was hard to separate his words from the rest of the holiday makers enjoying a drink in the sun. I was momentarily distracted by scents of melons, cucumbers, and coconut, transporting me back to high school pool parties.

"...just want what I'm owed."

The 10k, I guessed. The three of us looked at each other. It was so hard not to lean toward their table.

A pretty waitress who didn't look entirely old enough to be serving alcohol set down three coasters on our table, effectively ruining our mystery solving. "What can I get you?"

We spoke in unison, "A beer."

"Draft or bottle? We've got–"

Kevin cut her off with his almost breathless

answer. "Draft is fine. Something local, please and thank you."

She looked bemused, but she tapped quickly on her tablet. "I'll be back in a moment."

We turned our attention back to the next table, but the man had apparently had his say.

The woman's reply was much easier to hear. "Don't worry. I've got it in a safe place, Rusty, darling. I can give it to you once we're back on board, if it really can't wait."

Her voice had taken on a flirtatious quality, as though she were trying to wheedle the elusive Rusty into doing things her way.

A curse was all I could make out from his reply. Then a chair scraped against the concrete and Rusty's voice carried with a parting threat. "See that you do, Violet."

Three large glasses of beer were deposited on the table. We looked at each other and up at the waitress.

I pulled out some cash. "Will this cover it?"

The waitress nodded and plucked the bill from my hands. "I'll be right back with your change."

"No need, thank you."

She beamed. "Thank you!"

We took a minute to each have a long sip from our drinks– crime solving was thirsty work.

"Did you hear the way she said 'safe place?'" I asked Edie and Kevin. "I think she may have stored something in a safe. If it is someplace we can discover it, it must be with the purser."

"Then how about we head back to the ship and see what we can find? Beat her to it? And him..." Edie pointed, and Kevin and I turned to follow her gaze to none other than Coach coming up to the women with drinks.

"Hurry, before he gets something out of them!"

I wasn't sure we should go back so fast. "Shouldn't we interview them?"

"Not yet. Let's jump on this while it's hot."

I took one last drag on my beer and followed on Edie's surprisingly fast heels, taking a last glance over my shoulder at Coach and the women.

I hoped he'd hold them off long enough for us to find our next clue.

CHAPTER
TWELVE

We raced back to the ship, pausing only to dig around for the key cards that would be scanned at the top of the gangway before we could embark.

As Edie waded through the depths of her bag, I looked up to see a familiar snake-adorned bicep as Rusty, Violet's so-called 'friend' and potential hitman briskly strode up the gangway. I knew I only had a moment, so I didn't waste any time.

"Excuse me! Sir? Do you have a second?"

He looked at me like I had grown two heads.

I gave him my best smile. "I just wanted to ask you a few questions about Lucas Chalmers."

He stiffened slightly. "What about him?"

The thing about not wasting a moment before

jumping in is that sometimes a moment would be well spent considering a plan of action. Oh, well.

"Er, I mean, I guess I'd like to talk to you about his wife, Violet."

"I know who his wife is." He glared impatiently, not giving an inch. He was really taking his role seriously.

"Yes, I've heard. In fact, I've heard that you may have been helping her out with a problem she's been trying to solve. If you know what I mean?"

If his demeanor had seemed aggressively impatient before, well, now it was plain old aggressively aggressive. I took an involuntary step back out of his arm's reach.

"I don't know what you mean, but I do know you need to mind your own business, if you know what's good for you." He directed his stink eye at Edie and Kevin. "All three of you!" His muscles tightened as he spoke. He was really getting into his role.

He strode off without a backward glance.

I looked at Kevin and Edie. "He must be one of the professional actors they brought in for the weekend."

Edie watched him appreciatively until he was out of sight. "He's a ham, but I like a man who throws himself into his work." She wriggled her eyebrows a couple of times.

"Grandma, focus, we haven't got much time to solve this thing!" Kevin brought her back to the task at hand—solving Lucas' murder.

"Kevin is right. Rusty was a bust, but maybe we can get more out of Violet." I thrust my key card into the staff member's hand. He scanned my card and handed it back.

Edie had a quick word with the attendant, and I saw her slip him a twenty.

"You don't have to tip them for letting us back on board, Edie!"

She grinned broadly at my confusion and laughed. "To slow Coach down a little. It would be a shame if the system went down for a few minutes and no one's key cards would scan."

Mirth bubbled up in me like I was a little kid. "Remind me to never cross you."

Kevin and I laughed so hard, we had heads turning toward us at our arrival back on deck.

"Okay, let's hurry. I think we should check in with a man about a trolley."

We didn't need to consult on our next move. We went straight to see Brady and filled him in on what we overheard.

"So, do you think the purser might have something interesting in his safe?" I asked.

He grinned, making a show of slowly clapping his hands. "You're definitely on the right path, but you haven't solved it all just yet." He checked his watch. "Don't worry, you have a few more hours to go. By the way, you can find the purser at the Concierge Desk."

That reminder gave me a stomach drop. I wanted to solve this thing before the last second. Wanted it so bad I could taste it.

I just wished Shane had wanted it as bad, or rather, to be with me bad enough to endure the mystery weekend I'd planned. Having fun with Edie and Kevin was giving me all sorts of insights I didn't want to have.

I took out my phone and sent him a where-are-you? text, but no little dots popped up to show me he'd read my message. I sighed and focused back on the case, tuning back in to what Edie and Kevin were saying.

Kevin took charge of the conversation, steering Edie back on topic, away from Coach's involvement in riding our coattails to the facts as we had them so far.

"First, we know that Lucas was a hound, with

girls all over the place, including on board. So, his wife, Violet, wanted a divorce."

"But," Edie broke in, "she didn't want to lose his money or her family vacation home."

"And,' I added, "she did say she wanted Rusty to push him overboard. And we have motive, premeditation, even, and means. She's here on the ship, knows the ins and outs of the whole place. Not to mention, Rusty looked like he could be violent for cash, or fun." I recounted his little display at dinner when the server nearly brushed against him.

Edie and Kevin nodded along with me as I ticked off the list. Edie held up her hand, fingers splayed and started ticking off items herself.

"She's not the only woman on board who wanted him out of the way, though." Edie reminded us. "One, Angela wasn't too pleased that he got promoted over her for the Cruise Director job. And two, Angela was on the scene of the crime, which is means, opportunity, motive--"

I stopped her. "Is that motive enough? We know she wanted the job, but would she have killed for it?"

We looked at each other. It was hard to say. Some people could be ruthless, especially in a fictional murder mystery.

Kevin's gaze slid back and forth between the two of us. "Aren't you forgetting something?"

We both rounded on him. "What?"

"The girlfriend? We still don't have a name for her. And whatever is in the safe."

"He's right. Let's get there fast before they have time to get back onboard."

By now, we knew the quickest way to the Concierge Desk. We were there in no time flat.

There was an officious man behind the desk. He assessed our little party and finally settled his gaze on Edie. Lifting his chin and flaring his nostrils like he'd smelled something unpleasant, he let out a heavy sigh before asking, "Can I help you?"

Edie read him right away and put on her best no-nonsense voice. "Look here, sonny–"

Kevin gently cut her off. "What my grandmother is trying to say is, we think you may have something in the safe for the murder mystery participants."

The man didn't quite roll his eyes, but he clearly wasn't one of the staff excited to play along. "One moment."

He disappeared into the office behind him and quickly reappeared with an envelope.

We looked at each other. I don't know about

Edie or Kevin, but I had been expecting an object of some kind.

The concierge handed the envelope to Kevin. "Happy hunting."

He could not have sounded more bored. I thanked him and held a breath as the three of us stared at the envelope.

Apparently, we were in the concierge's way. He sighed again and asked, "Is there anything else I can do for you?"

"No." Edie grabbed the clue and tore it open.

But his question prompted my brain. I remembered that I was supposed to collect my casino winnings. "Actually, second thought," I smiled politely, "I won at roulette yesterday. Could I withdraw some from my account, please?"

He straightened up, back into professional mode. "May I have your key card?"

I handed it over, and he swiped it. "Name?"

"Watson. Mia Watson." He tapped it in and looked at the monitor and then at me. "You have a balance of one thousand dollars and twenty-two cents. Would you like that in cash or perhaps you would like to do a little shopping while you're onboard? We have some lovely boutiques." I ignored the meaningful eye he cast over my outfit.

"What? Why is the balance only a thousand dollars? That's at least five hundred dollars less than my winnings!"

He looked at his monitor again. "Let me see. Your account has a two hundred and thirty-five dollar bar tab, and the remainder of three-forty-two-fifty was used this morning in the jewelry shop. Is there a problem?"

"Yes, absolutely there is!" My heart beat out an SOS code as I asked, "Which way is the jewelry shop from here?"

I barely registered his directions, allowing Edie and Kevin to pull me along. We rushed straight to the jewelry shop. With a real crime to solve, murder was temporarily on the back burner. I would deal with Shane later. Had he been drinking thirty-year-old single malt?

The jeweler was quite understanding and showed us the receipt for an expensive necklace.

Edie clapped her hands. "An anniversary present!"

I considered it. "Maybe. He has been a pill this trip. He's usually not one for showy gifts, but he did say he'd try harder." Actually, I wasn't at all sure what he mumbled in my general direction, but he sure needed to try harder. Maybe he thought I would overlook his bar tab if he spent the same amount on a gift.

"Ooh, how exciting! An I'm-sorry present from a man is usually the best kind."

"Ha. You're right. I'll ask Shane about it. When I can get in touch with him." I tried to hide my annoyance and turn off my what-iffing mind. "One mystery at a time. Let's focus on solving the case for now."

I looked at the jeweler. "How well did you know the Cruise Director, Lucas Chalmers?"

A sly grin made its way across her face. "Lucas is a very good customer. Very good." She adopted an appropriately mournful expression. "Was, I mean, of course. I can't believe he's gone. It's tragic."

"Of course." I tried not to wink, but a small one may have involuntarily happened.

"How good is very good? Do you mean he bought a lot of jewelry from you or that the two of you were having an affair?" As usual, Edie cut straight to the heart of the matter.

The young woman chuckled. "No, not me, ma'am. Not my type. I only meant that he is, *was*, a generous man."

"How generous?" We all wanted to know.

"Well, I can't give you details, you understand,

but I can say that just a few days ago, he picked up two beautiful pieces with custom engravings."

We leaned in a bit closer, and I lowered my voice. "Could you tell us what the engravings say, please?"

Edie slapped my arm. "What she meant was, 'Who is the jewelry for?'"

That got a laugh from the jeweler. She glanced around, then leaned in close and whispered, "All I can say is, I gave him two identical diamond necklaces with messages to two different women."

I gasped. "Kevin, Kevin, oh my gosh. I bet that was from the necklace. The diamond in the blood."

Kevin's eyes widened, and he took out the camera, going to the photo we'd examined last night. He showed it to the girl. "Would you recognize a diamond from the necklaces?"

The girl leaned over and scrunched up her nose. "I don't know, probably not. A diamond's a diamond. Unless it's paste." She straightened up and looked around again.

Edie and I exchanged a look. I guess she wasn't working on commission, or maybe the clerks rotated around all of the shops, and whoever happened to be on duty had to follow the script.

"Will there be anything else I can help you with today? Perhaps a nice watch for you, sir?"

"Yeah, Grandma, how about it?" Kevin glanced at the extravagant watches and chuckled at the prices. "Who doesn't need a thousand dollar watch?"

"You, that's who!" Edie cackled, never looking away from the cashier. "Maybe when he graduates with his Masters! Thank you for your help, dear. Maybe when this is over, you and Kevin will have time to get to know each other a little better."

Kevin groaned quietly.

The three of us left the store and ended up standing on the deck looking at one another for direction.

Kevin deferred to us. "Where to next?"

I was still stuck on the jewelry. "If my husband were to buy another woman a piece of jewelry, I might be tempted to kill him. Especially if he couldn't even be bothered to pick out individual pieces they might like. How lazy!"

Edie chimed in, "On the other hand, a woman who thinks her lover is about to leave his wife for her, may find that more difficult to believe, if he is still buying his wife jewelry."

Kevin and I looked at each other and mouthed, "Lover."

Our debate was cut short as we all clammed up at the sight of Coach stalking into the jewelry store. He saw Edie and made a beeline over to us.

He stood in front of Edie and pointed a finger in her bemused face. "Don't think I don't know you're to blame."

Edie batted her eyes. "Why, whatever for, Mr. Winston?"

"Don't play innocent."

"Couldn't if I tried, honey." Edie gave him an exaggerated wink as she channeled Mae West.

Coach lapsed from his mean face into a grin, but he quickly recovered and switched to pointing his finger at me. "I was going to trade information with you. Got something I know you don't. Got it straight from the horse's mouth."

I hated to take the bait, but I needed to know if he'd actually one-upped us. "What horse?"

Coach crossed his arms. "I talked to the girl-friend. Got a good lead. I'm willing to trade, but this time, you first. What do you know? I heard you ask about the tattoo guy."

I was impressed. He'd managed to talk the woman into sharing a clue, it seemed, and eavesdrop on us unseen. Edie and Kevin had equally surprised faces.

I uncrossed my own arms, trying to stop mirroring Coach's body language, and held out my hand. "Truce then, no tricks?"

Edie started to push my hand away and thought better of it. The look she gave me questioned my sanity, but she stayed quiet while Coach considered my offer.

"Truce." He shook my hand and recrossed his burly arms. "Go on then."

I let out a long breath. "Lucas seems to have had some shady dealings with the man with a snake tattoo. We found a clue that led us offshore to a bar where we were warned away. We came back here because we overheard the wife say something that led us here, to the jewelry store. Your turn."

Coach scanned our faces for lies. He must have been satisfied. "Okay. And what did you find here?"

Considering his interrogation techniques, I figured this information would save him quite a bit of time, but I was willing to add it for info on the girlfriend. "He got two identical pieces engraved here for two women—I'm assuming the wife and girlfriend..." I trailed off.

Coach relaxed at that information. "Oh, yeah,

you betcha. I'm sure it was for the wife and girl-friend. I talked to them both at the bar on shore today. Violet and Crystal seem a little too cozy for grieving widows or whatnot."

He stopped for a moment. "Now that you mention it, the girlfriend was wearing an expensive necklace. That could have been one of the gifts from Lucas."

Edie slapped her hands together. "And if one of them has a necklace and the other doesn't, maybe that means the other one is our killer! The neck-lace is a clue! The wife did it, surely. She lost a diamond from it in the struggle of the murder, and now she can't wear it or she'll reveal herself. Huh?"

Maybe that was it, maybe it was that simple. At least now we knew who the girlfriend was. I knew the woman with Lucas' wife looked familiar. She was the girlfriend, and she'd been lurking on the periphery of our investigation all along.

Edie wanted to break into the wife's room and see if we could find her matching necklace, but I wasn't sure we were supposed to go that far. Besides, we still had to see what was in the safe. Maybe the damning necklace was in there!

I raced back over to the counter and motioned to

the jeweler. "Where else on the ship would we find a safe?"

"Besides here?" The girl thought a moment. "All the state rooms have small safes, but the big ones are here in the shop and the Concierge Desk."

Well, we had already gotten our clue from the concierge. I looked at the other two. "The necklace could be in there." I addressed the girl again, "Know anywhere else that has a safe?"

She paused and thought for a moment. "There's the big one in the cruise director's office. He shares his office with the security team. They keep weapons and stuff in there, bigger things. No valuables though."

We all looked at each other. "Lucas's office!"

CHAPTER
THIRTEEN

We booked it for the elevator and were in luck. One was just arriving, and it was empty. As we descended, I saw a familiar bathing suit and sarong.

"Violet! Stop the elevator! We have to get off!"

Kevin quickly jabbed the button for the next floor. We raced back up the stairs, hoping Violet would still be there. Well, Kevin raced. Edie and I climbed the stairs as fast as we could. One thing was for sure, I needed to get in better shape before I did another of these murder mystery weekends.

Kevin was able to catch up to her. She probably couldn't walk very fast in the strappy heels she was wearing.

I shuddered to think what her feet must feel like

after traipsing around the island all day. My feet were still unhappy after a few hours in far more sensible heels than the night before.

I heard Violet's voice. "I'm sorry, I'm really not sure what I can help you with."

Kevin had clearly started without us, but Edie was determined to get her words in edgewise, too.

"Tell us about Lucas!" Edie demanded.

Violet started. I didn't think Edie had spoken that aggressively. Clearly, Violet needed a softer touch, but time was running out.

We were under the gun, so to speak, so I went for broke. "What about your cherished family summer home?"

I was hoping quoting the words from the script would get a reaction from her, and it did, but not the one I expected. Her shoulders relaxed.

"The summer home! Of course! It's been in my family for years." She seemed oddly giddy, not the excitement of the staff roped in to answer questions, but nervous relief.

I looked at Edie and Kevin, and back at Violet. "So, you weren't worried that Lucas might get the house in your divorce?"

"Oh, right, I mean, I could have definitely bene-fited from his death. You know, he's, he was, such a player. He made me so angry. All the time. Fooling around right under my face with every woman he knew." Violet was babbling now, her demeanor completely changed from a moment earlier. She definitely wasn't one of the professional actors.

I pressed on, since she was clearly in a mood to talk. "Is this a confession?" I looked over at Edie and Kevin in disbelief and disappointment. This was kind of a letdown after all of our running around.

Violet giggled. "Well, I can't say that I had anything to do with the murder. Too gnarly for me. But it's been so fun talking to you. Great interrogation! I've got to go now. Laters!" She pivoted on one pointed heel and sashayed past me. I got a whiff of an iconic 90s scent as she passed.

Cucumbers and melons and high school all hit my hippocampus with a punch of nostalgia. But it also made me think that our not-so-shrinking Violet was stuck in the past, perhaps. Explained her wardrobe and lingo.

What had just happened?

"What the heck was that?" Edie broke the silence. "Is she getting paid? Does she know about acting classes?"

"I think she may have been hired for her ability to walk around the island in a bikini and heels."

Kevin opined. "You don't see many MILFs that look like her. She's got the look of a—"

"Teenager?" I supplied.

Edie playfully slapped Kevin's hand and raised an eyebrow at me. "Now, you two, don't judge a book by its cover. It's what's on the inside that counts."

Kevin and I both laughed at those words coming from Edie's mouth.

I shooed the pair into action. "We can talk about MILFs and strength of character later. We've still got to get to Lucas' office. We've already wasted enough time with Violet. Let's go!"

Despite the detour, we were at Lucas' office in under ten minutes. Not bad, considering how large the ship was and how long our little chat had taken.

Kevin pushed open the door, and we all gasped.

Lucas' assistant, Angela, was ransacking the room.

As soon as we made eye contact, Angela ran out, leaving behind an office in chaos. The cruise director half, at any rate. What was presumably the security officers' side was neat and tidy.

Kevin turned to follow her–he could run faster than we could. Edie and I stayed to survey the damage and see if Angela had left any clues for us.

"What do we have here?" Edie held up a shred of paper. "I'll wager this is our big break!"

I came over to her side, eager to see what she'd found.

"Where was it?"

"It was lying there on the table." Edie pointed to the nightstand and then flicked the paper in her hand. I noticed that the note had been scribbled on what looked like the remnants of a flyer.

We examined it closer.

My gaze landed on exactly what we needed. "Look!"

Edie nodded. "An address. Perfect."

I pulled out my phone and typed the address into a map app. It was a museum on the other side of the island.

I checked the time. "If we hurry, we'll have one hour on shore before the gangway is pulled in!"

We ran like Forrest Gump all the way to the gangway, but I had a niggling feeling we were being sent on a wild goose chase. The sound of laughter somewhere above us stopped me in my tracks. I looked up to see Coach leaning over a rail above us. He saw me and waved from the upper deck, his laughter making up my mind.

I halted Edie and Kevin, too. We were halfway

down the gangway already, and I was going on a gut feeling that we shouldn't leave the boat. It had to be a fool's errand.

"What does Coach know that we don't?" I asked, jerking my head to where he stood up above.

Edie followed my scowl, her face quickly mirroring mine.

"That little--" she stopped and shook her fist at him. "No dancing for you tonight."

I half-laughed, but the other half of me was worried. "What do you two think? Should we try to get to the museum, or should we follow Coach and find out what he knows?"

"Coach!" Kevin didn't hesitate.

Edie swatted his arm. "The museum! It was a clue from Angela. Coach could be bluffing."

I went with my gut and cast the deciding vote. "Coach."

We turned back up the gangway and impatiently waited for our key cards to be scanned again. Why were we being held up? We hadn't even really left! Finally, we were admitted back onto the ship. We headed straight for the elevators to take us to the upper deck, where Coach had been waving at us.

Kevin spotted Coach's purple and gold cap disappearing as the glass elevator sank out of sight.

"He's going deeper below deck!" Kevin urged us to move faster. We stepped into our own elevator and surveyed our options. Kevin pushed a button decisively. "Where is he headed? The ship's night-club is the only place to go to relax in this direction."

The elevators were all going up, and we couldn't stand around waiting for them to come back down. Reluctantly, we took the stairs. When we finally pulled open the heavy doors to the night-club, sure enough, there was Coach. Once again, he was trying to intimidate Angela into giving him information.

Angela didn't back down. She stood tall, her eyes flashing. "I don't know what you're talking about. You're taking this all a bit too seriously. I'm just playing my character in the game."

Coach sneered. "Save it, sweetheart. I know you're mixed up in something big."

"Chill out. This is supposed to be fun, remember?" I tugged his arm, hoping he would back away from her. You could cut the tension in the room with a knife.

Suddenly, Angela pushed her way past Coach to the door. "You can't just come in here and threaten me!"

Coach lunged for her, but Kevin stepped in front

of Angela, shielding her. "Back off, man. We're not afraid of you."

The two men stood there, locked in a tense standoff. My heart pounded, the adrenaline coursing through my veins like my blood was on a high-speed chase to my chest.

Edie grabbed my hand and squeezed it tight, facing Coach.

"Leave my grandson alone!" Her voice shook a little, but her words were loud and clear.

"You three don't know what you're talking about. There's more to this than meets the eye." Coach gave her a long look, then turned and walked away.

We all took a deep breath and released it at the same time. Angela was still shaking, and Kevin was still standing protectively in front of her. I couldn't help but feel a sense of admiration for him. He was always the first to step up and protect those around him.

"Are you okay?" I asked Angela.

She nodded. "Yeah, thanks to you guys."

As the four of us walked away from the club, I couldn't shake the feeling that there was something more to this game than just harmless fun. Coach was too intense, and Angela was too scared. I made a decision then and there that I was going to get to the bottom of this, no matter what it took.

My phone buzzed gently in my pocket. Pulling it out, I saw a text from Shane.

Hey, babe. How's the game going?

I hesitated for a moment, unsure of what to say. The truth was, we were knee deep in the real-life mystery of why Coach was being so weird, and I wasn't sure what was going to happen next. But I wouldn't worry him unnecessarily, so I typed out a casual response.

Game's going great! Having a blast. Miss you though.

I hit send and slipped my phone back into my pocket. There was no turning back now. We were in too deep. But I had a feeling that, with my team by my side, we could solve this mystery and come out on top.

By the time the four of us got to the elevator, steam was coming from Edie's ears. "Can you believe I was going to canoodle with him tonight?!" She pulled her bag off one arm and hitched it firmly onto her other shoulder. "I'm sorry, Mia, but you're going to have to carry on alone for a few minutes. Kevin, you're with me!"

She looked at her grandson. "I need a word with

Mr. Winston. You come with me in case he has any ideas of speaking to me with the tone he was using with Angela."

Kevin needed to work on his poker face because he clearly thought that was a bad idea.

"Time's a'wasting! Mia will be fine without us for a couple of minutes. Let's go!" She turned back to the nightclub and strode off with more pep in her step than she had had all day.

The elevator door opened and Angela stepped in. I hesitated, then got on with her. It had been a while since anyone had shown such confidence in me. I wasn't going to let Edie down.

"Are you sure you're okay, Angela?" I was genuinely concerned. She still seemed rattled by the encounter. "Coach, er, Mr. Winston, can be cantankerous." Not usually to this degree, but I kept that to myself.

"I'm fine. Really. Thank you for asking. Are you enjoying the murder mystery weekend?" Angela's shoulders relaxed slightly, but her smile didn't quite meet her eyes.

"I'm having a blast! Edie and Kevin are great fun, and the three of us make a good team."

"Have you known each other long?"

"Um, no, actually, I planned to participate with

my husband, but he–" I shrugged and let my sentence trail off. "Anyway, Edie and Kevin and I hit it off right away. So, I've been working with them."

The elevator doors opened and Angela wished me luck solving Lucas' murder before she stepped out.

I followed her. "Before you go, would you mind if I asked you a few questions about your relationship with Lucas?"

Angela looked at her phone. "Actually, I'm running late. Maybe later?" She smiled apologetically.

I sped up to keep pace with her. No way was I letting her slip through my fingers now.

"Just a couple of questions." Angela didn't respond, so I dove right in. "I heard that Lucas was promoted over you. How did that make you feel?"

She gave me a wry grin, but didn't slow down. "How do you think I felt? I trained him." She shook her head. "He didn't promote himself, if you think I might have killed him over it."

"No, but with Lucas out of the way, you're next in line."

"Actually, I'm still an Assistant Cruise Director. There isn't a line of succession." She chuckled

ruefully. "Otherwise, I might have been tempted."
She winked as she opened the doors to the galley.

There went her motive. No ladder to climb, no
reason to kill.

Still, questioning her might prove useful. I took a
quick peek in the galley. No knife-wielding chef in
sight. I slipped in along with her. If she was
surprised, she didn't say anything.

I took my opening. "I don't suppose you have
any opinions on who it might have been, then?"

"That would be cheating, and there's no glory in
that." Her words were softened with another quick
smile, one that reached all the way to her eyes. "I'm
afraid I've got to go now."

"Just one more question!" I begged, a little
louder than necessary considering I was in a staff-
only area. "What do you know about the relationship between Lucas' wife and his girlfriend? And
what does Rusty have to do with it?"

"That's two questions. One, Lucas was seeing a
lot of girls, so which girlfriend do you mean? Two,
Rusty is a whipped pup for Violet. He'd do anything
for her. Anything."

"Wait, how many girls?"

Angela shrugged and looked at her watch, a pink
old school wristwatch with a face surrounded by as

much bling as her perfect nails. "And I'm out of time." She strode off, weaving through the galley staff, who barely seemed to register our presence.

I looked down the row of men and women prepping plates on the long worktop and the dance of tray-laden servers carefully avoiding one another. I followed Angela as quickly as I could, ducking to avoid trays.

"Mise en place!"

My head jerked toward the familiar voice as the command rang out. *No, no, no!* I looked around for an escape route. I didn't want to be back on the wrong end of the chef's knife.

A row of trolleys were laid out for room service, draped with brilliant white tablecloths just like the trolley Brady had been pushing the first time I saw him. I dipped my head to avoid eye contact, quickly edged through the servers to the nearest trolley, and dropped to a squat. I ducked under the tablecloth and climbed rather inelegantly onto the low shelf.

How was I going to know when the coast was clear? Ugh. I needed to get out of here, but I also wanted to avoid getting caught.

I didn't have time to give it another thought, because a tray was deposited above me and the brake was kicked up. The server gave the trolley a

GWEN TAYLOR & JEN BOOKER

pull, grunted, kicked the brake again, in case it hadn't disengaged, and heaved the cart into motion with a swear. I winced as the galley doors were rammed apart.

The trolley stopped a moment later, presumably for the elevator. I lifted the hem and stopped.

Gold! Of course!

I eased my way out from under the trolley, praying I didn't catch the tablecloth and bring the tray down on myself.

"What the--" the server uttered a few curses of surprise.

"Sorry. I'm here for the murder. Must've gotten lost. Thanks! Don't tell anyone."

I gave the server an apologetic smile and hurried off, hoping he wasn't going to report me to anyone. Angela may not have had much to say, but I had learned something—how the killer got in and out of the scene of the crime and also why there'd been no evidence before. We'd had the wrong trolley. The detail that had been nagging at me had finally clicked. There was no gold hem on the one we inspected.

If Edie was done giving Coach a piece of her mind, we needed to find that trolley.

CHAPTER
FOURTEEN

The three of us raced back to the scene of the crime. I took in the determination on Edie's and Kevin's faces. I knew mine looked the same, with maybe a little more anxiety tossed in. We knew we were running out of time. I'd so wanted to break that record Brady had mentioned, or at the least, win the prize.

I felt like I'd let him down, not solving this sooner, and when we finally found him, I was suddenly a bit shy.

"Hi," I panted, stooping to put my hands on my knees and take a few breaths before going on. "We need to talk."

"Oh, that is never a good opener. What's up?"

"Trolley, you...switched." I bent back over and breathed a bit more shallow and slow.

Edie took over and asked Brady for the trolley he had when he found the body, hoping to find some clue the murderer had left behind.

"Follow me, sleuths." He smiled broadly and led us to his office, where we found one trolley with a gold trim on its tablecloth. Under that all-important tablecloth, on the trolley's lower shelf was a keyring, with a single key on it.

The three of us looked at one another. An actual door key? It was too large to be meant for luggage or a padlock.

I thought back to where I had seen a single corridor that hadn't been converted to electronic keys while we had been looking for 'places to relax'. "I know where this goes! Follow me."

It didn't take us long to get there, but a single corridor on a ship still has a lot of doors. I sighed. There was nothing to do but try them one by one until we found the lock that matched the key.

We tried door after door. No luck. We reached the last door. One more chance.

Surely we hadn't wasted our last few minutes. There weren't many places I had seen onboard with actual door keys. Kevin hesitated at the lock.

"One more chance. What if we've been looking in the wrong place?"

"Pshaw, give me that." Edie grabbed the key from Kevin, jammed it in the slot, and gave it a firm twist.

We pushed the door open to find Angela waiting for us.

She was all smiles as she checked her watch. "Record time to find the murder weapon! Congratulations, players!"

We thanked her, reaching out as she handed over a small Zemi statue just the right size to fit on the bare plinth. It had a red sticker on it, to represent the blood from the murder, I supposed.

Angela reached back out, pulling the red sticker off with her blingy nails. "Don't know why that's on there. Ruins the wood."

I eyed her sparkly nails and dazzling watch and met her gaze. "Thank you. Good idea."

Edie squealed and squeezed my arm. "This is it! It wasn't a crime of passion, after all. Talk about a big red herring."

I sighed. "Hold that thought, Edie."

"Why? We actually did it! But we have to go give a breakdown of the murder to the captain before we can take home the prize."

I sobered up. "Yes, and I have something to tell you on the way. But first, we have to get to the finish line and wrap this up. Let's go!"

With our prize in hand, we rushed back to the scene of the crime to clock in and explain how we solved the mystery before any of the other participants beat us to it, with or without the evidence.

Edie and I dug deep to keep up the pace as Kevin glided down the corridor and up the stairs like a gazelle. As Edie and I passed the bar, I slowed down, and not because I was out of breath. Well, not only because I was out of breath. I knew the woman at the cafe looked familiar!

The woman Coach had told us was named Crystal, the same one who'd been having drinks at the café onshore with when we followed Rusty, sauntered past us, still wearing the same bikini and sarong. . . and a very expensive necklace.

CHAPTER
FIFTEEN

Edie, Kevin, and I arrived at the event room just as the clock started to chime, announcing the end of the murder mystery event.

"We know what happened!" I huffed, trying to catch my breath.

The crowded room settled immediately. You could hear a pin drop. All eyes were on the three of us and the Zemi statue in Kevin's hands.

Kevin had seemingly made the mad dash without the slightest effort. He picked up where I left off with my quiet wheezing. "The assistant cruise director Angela is the murderer!"

"And she had help. The trolley man!" He pointed at Brady. "He helped her avoid being seen near

Lucas' body by giving her a ride out on the trolley. She was hiding under the tablecloth that conveniently went below the shelf underneath."

"Back up!" I stopped Kevin. He looked around as though I meant for him to move. "No, I mean, you haven't started at the beginning."

Kevin dipped his head and gestured for me to continue.

"While the Captain rallied everyone to the muster drill, Angela and Lucas had a public argument that ended with Angela pushing him. The two of them share an office, so why would they have chosen such a public spot in front of all of us to quarrel?" I looked around at the crowd. "It was the first clue!"

Several weekend sleuths groaned and muttered to themselves.

Edie picked up where Kevin had left off. "Exactly so. After the murder, as my grandson was explaining, Brown Eyes, er, Brady switched trolleys. The one we saw in the storage room had a golden trim, but the one he showed all of us at the pool was pure white. They switched them!"

Kevin lifted up his camera like he might show the crime scene photos and then thought better of it. He added, "Yeah, and she must have had a flashlight, so she could see once the lights were out and the door to the back room was closed. She probably slipped in the back room as soon as the lights went out."

I piped up with the murder weapon clue. "Once the storage room door was closed, she clobbered Lucas with the Zemi statue from the plinth."

We let that sink in for a moment before Edie dropped the next clue. "And she took the very valuable, and now blood-stained, relic with her, but she dropped her key! She tried to throw us off the scent, saying she wouldn't be promoted even if Lucas died, but we followed the evidence." Edie shook a finger in Angela's direction, as though scolding her.

I butted in. "Because losing the promotion wasn't her motive. It had nothing to do with the promotion. She was Lucas' lover too."

Several of the other sleuths gasped loudly this time. Maybe no one else had gone down this line of thinking. I continued. "There was a diamond in the blood, or what looked like one. And we thought it came from the wife's necklace, but it wasn't a diamond. It was paste. A rhinestone. From her rhinestone watch."

Edie took the last line. "It was a crime of passion after all, of an affair we all got to see ending as we filed into the ballroom. And like his wife told us all, I'm sure, Lucas had a thing with every woman he knew."

Several of the mystery weekenders nodded. Someone started a slow clap until the whole room erupted in applause.

Lucas strolled into the room in the middle of it and spread his arms like the clapping was for him. He must have been listening from just outside the door, because as soon as he reached the front of the room and the clapping ceased, he announced that we had correctly solved the mystery.

"Ladies and gentlemen," he paused at the spattering of applause, "our players here have won the two-week cruise aboard the Bella Blanca with all amenities included. And this lovely replica statue as a memento of their victory. Well done, folks." He passed the statue to Edie, who curtsied to the crowd and then handed it to me with a bow.

"It's yours, dear. You take it. You figured out the golden thread and the real motive."

"Thank you, Edie. I'll treasure it." Tears welled up in my eyes. I was going to miss my new friends something fierce after tomorrow. I held it up like a trophy to the crowd.

More applause sounded now and Edie waved at

the crowd like a pro. Lucas quieted the audience down again and continued. "And..."

From the crowd, a surly murder mystery sore loser yelled, "Get on with it!"

A tittering of laughter made Lucas smile. "Fair enough, fair enough. And they won dinner tonight at the Captain's table. Cheers to our fine players, all of you, and let's give our employee-players a hand, please." Lucas pointed each person out in turn. "Angela, my very capable assistant, Sam, the bartender, Svetlana, the croupier, Pierre, the concierge, and Valentina, the masseuse answered your questions while carrying out their regular duties. Brady, our head of security, played your friendly caterer this weekend, and Violet, one of our dancers, who played my long-suffering wife."

We all gave them a long round of applause. Once the clapping petered out, Lucas introduced the remaining players.

"Of course, we couldn't have done this without professional help. Professional actors, I mean. Let's hear it for Rusty, who played the part of the would-be hitman, and Crystal, who played the part of my impatient mistress. Please come up and take a bow!"

I leaned over to Edie. "I was half-expecting Coach to be one of the players, you know."

She looked at me in surprise. "Coach?"

"The way he got in Angela's face, giving her the third degree, like a real crime had been committed."

The actors had all assembled before us and were looking to Lucas for their cue, but he was looking at me. I waved my prize and clapped and he snapped back to attention.

"Everyone, please, take a bow! A round of applause for our dedicated actors!"

They all stepped up, joining hands and bowing. The women raised their clasped hands high, and Crystal pressed the necklace against her throat as they took another bow.

I stopped clapping, a clue I'd overlooked suddenly stared me in the face.

Without a word, I pushed the statue into Kevin's surprised arms, turned, and headed for the bar.

As I suspected, I found my husband in the bar where he has spent most of the trip. I steeled my spine. I was about to do the one thing my momma said never to do.

Make a scene.

"You did buy a necklace, didn't you? With my casino winnings. You just didn't buy it for me."

Shane looked panicked. "What are you going on about?"

I turned to the woman walking up to join him. Lucas's pretend mistress.

And the real mistress to my own husband. Crystal.

She sat, putting her hand possessively on my

husband's arm. "I guess we don't need to pretend anymore. Do we, honey bunny?"

My husband looked trapped, and his mouth was moving, but no sound came out.

I felt like I'd become a statue watching this play out.

All the things you think you'd feel in this moment, things maybe you'd think of what-iffing, none of that came.

I was calm. I was actually more than calm. I was done.

Done with neglect, done with overlooking real-world clues just to hang on to something that was toxic to the happiness I needed in my life.

Shane was finally uttering words, but I wasn't processing them.

"Mia!"

Jolted from my stasis, I turned to see Edie and Kevin joining me. They stood, one on either side of me. And then Brady joined, a guilty look on his face as he realized what I was seeing. And I had a realization of my own. The clue he'd dropped at dinner. He'd seen them together. He'd seen Shane dancing. And so had I! That had been him when I thought I was seeing things.

I was the last to know. Well, the last to finally accept it, maybe.

I took a deep breath and faced the man I didn't know at all and the woman he'd brought on our anniversary trip. "He's all yours."

Shane sputtered, "Mia, wait."

"Let her go," Crystal said.

She actually lifted the glass he had waiting for her in a mock toast and smiled, her expensive manicure flicking against the necklace bought with my money. That did make me mad.

I had the wild urge to tear it from her neck.

Brady seemed to anticipate my desire and approached her, pulling out his security badge and flashing it in front of her smug face.

"Ma'am, that's stolen property around your neck. Unless you want to be implicated in the theft and have your employment terminated, I suggest you hand it over."

Stunned, Crystal complied, her grin even more smug as she said, "I was only hired for the murder mystery, anyway. To surprise Shaney-poo on his trip."

Edie made a loud gagging noise.

Lucas passed the necklace to me with a smug grin of his own. "Your property, Miss Watson."

I took the necklace that I'd sure as heck be returning and spoke to my husband what felt like the final words of our marriage. "Happy anniversary."

"Mia! No, we can fix this. It's not--" Shane started toward me and grabbed my arm roughly, but Brady towered over him with a firm command, pulling me from Shane's grasp and gesturing for me to get behind him.

"Don't even think about it."

I turned before Shane could see the tears welling in my eyes. Standing around me were my new friends, Edie, Kevin, Brady. They wrapped me in a group hug.

Edie pushed the others away, dragging me along, back toward the jewelry store and the cabins. "Let's cash that in and cash you out before she realizes there's no investigation."

I glanced up at Brady and smiled through the tears waiting to fall. "Thank you. All of you."

"Let's get your stuff from your room. You're staying with us until departure time. And then we need to get you something hard to drink and talk bad about those two til morning." Edie gave me the tightest hug that I didn't know I needed. It felt like her arms were all that were holding me together right now.

Brady said a short goodbye and left me with my two conspirators, saying he'd check in later, but I'm not sure that was meant for me or Edie. But she waved him off and pushed Kevin along as well.

I was feeling like a shock victim. I wasn't processing what had just happened to me. I was merely moving my feet as Edie led me away from life as I'd known it.

The stores and restaurants were a slow-mo tour as I started to feel a deep panic in my chest about the end of my marriage.

"Oh god, what will I do?" I practically wailed to Edie.

"You'll get your money and your life back is what you'll do. Starting here."

We rounded the corner of the deck and came to stand in front of the jewelry store.

"It's going to be okay, I promise, dear."

I squeezed Edie's hand. "Is it? People always say that, but--"

"No but's. First, money, then we tackle the rest of your life. Your new life. You, me, Kevin, maybe that handsome Brady boy, and a ship full of promise. You got this. *We* got this."

Edie gave me a concerned look. "Unless you want to fix things..." she trailed off, not saying what she thought about fixing it. But it was written on her face.

I shook my head. "No, I don't think there's any fixing this." My chest tightened with the epiphanies flooding my mind. "It's over."

The tears unleashed then, and I was glad for Edie holding me up when my legs felt like they might give way.

A few feet away, Kevin rocked on the balls of his feet, clearly uncomfortable and wanting to get away. He caught me staring at him and offered to help. "Want me to go in for you?"

I blinked, unwilling to go into the store a sobbing mess, and shook my head. I lifted a shaking hand to the door. "No. Edie was right." I straightened my clothes, wiped my tears off, and took a deep breath. "I've got this."

CHAPTER

SEVENTEEN

I sat alone in the bargain cabin that had been booked to celebrate my marriage and now had seen the end of it. Needless to say, I was not too keen on going back out onto the busy decks.

Most of the weekenders had disembarked hours ago and now the new passengers were milling about the ship like a swarm of excited ants with a taste for sunscreen and shuffleboard.

My bags were packed, considerably lighter now that half the clothes it had carried had gone ashore with my husband and his mistress—my replacement, for the time being, at least. She hadn't taken his promises to work things out with me very well. I suspected, one way or another, that relationship would not last long.

I had one half-empty suitcase and my travel beach bag where the little statue we'd won in the contest was nestled inside a beach towel to keep it from breaking.

It already had a scratch on it from where Kevin dressed it up with his sunglasses and nicked it trying to remove them after a few drinks last night. Both Kevin and the statue had ended up in the floor face down. I'm surprised it wasn't broken. The base looked a little damaged, like there was a crack in it, but it was safe now. As the only gift I'd gotten on my own anniversary trip, and a memento of my sleuthing achievement, I wasn't about to let it suffer any more damage. I was going to give it a place of honor. Let it serve as a reminder that I could win at something.

I still couldn't believe the turn my life had taken on a dime. Mere days, hours earlier, I was celebrating my fifteenth anniversary.

Now, I was heading home. Alone. My husband had already gone on to his new life with his new love, although he'd texted, saying we should talk. Some of his messages started with 'We can fix this,' but I'd ignored them and him. He'd even told me that Crystal had surprised him by auditioning for the role, like that made it better somehow. I had nothing to say to that, so I'd avoided talking to him at all, using Edie and Kevin like bouncers.

They'd let me stay in their cabin suite, in Edie's room, until Shane had cleared out this morning. Now I was back in here, doing the cleaning up of our cabin and my life before going home.

A laugh suddenly burst out of me. Home. Where was that even at? Home? Did I have one to go back to? The thought had been swirling in my mind all night. Where would I go?

At least I had my laptop. Not that I'd done any writing on this trip. I realized I hadn't been able to write romance in what felt like ages because I no longer knew what it looked like, sounded like, felt like.

Maybe I was finished as a writer, just like Shane had said. Or maybe I just needed a fresh start. Despite the uncertainties of my future, I was feeling lighter than I had in years.

I picked up my single suitcase, single in more ways than one. I sighed, and left my old room behind, headed for the gangway. I'd have to face my new life and my old friends back home sooner or later. Did they already know? Had Shane already introduced our friends to my replacement? I didn't want to think about it.

"Mia! Stop!"

I turned at the bridge.

Edie came racing up to me, dragging Brady with her. "Tell her. Go on."

I blinked quickly a few times to dispel the tears in my eyes and squinted at them. "Tell me what?"

What fresh ill was it now? Had Shane bought something else for his tart and left me to settle the bill?

Brady handed me a piece of official looking paper. "Your friend here seems to think you'd go for this. I figured it was worth a shot, too."

I glanced down at the document. The top read *Application*.

It was already filled out. With my name, at least. In a masculine block letter style.

The paper shook in my already trembling hands. "I'm sorry. I'm confused."

Edie pushed the paper up in my hands closer to my face, like seeing it was my problem. She tapped the section where it said 'The successful candidate will...' and laughed. "There's a job opening. Here, on the ship. And one I've convinced the Captain and Brady that you're perfect for."

I focused on the application. Assistant Cruise Director.

I looked up at Brady, sure I resembled a confused puppy. "Isn't that Angela's job?"

He shook his head. "Not anymore. She's now Cruise Director. This was Lucas' last voyage with us."

"I don't know anything about directing... anything!" My head swam. Could I? Should I? "Besides, how long does it even take to interview and decide--"

Brady cut me off. "As of right now, there are no other candidates, and I have a little something to say about who takes the position."

Edie and Brady stared at me, waiting for me to say something.

I had no idea what to say.

I glanced over at the gangway. People were coming, some going, all looking happier than I felt, all heading on to new adventures.

Maybe...

"Maybe you can apply, try it on a temporary basis if you'd rather look at it that way. You can leave anytime, and I'll keep looking for a permanent candidate. Since Lucas is leaving us in a bind, we have some leeway here."

"Well, I--"

"That's it, come on," Edie cajoled. "You miss all

the chances you don't take. Besides, you said your-self last night that you hated to say goodbye to me and Kevin. This way, you don't have to. You can share in our adventure until you find your own."

The tears came flooding back. "Oh, Edie."

I hugged the older woman who was fast becoming one of the best friends I'd ever had.

"Go on with you." She wiped at her own eyes as she pulled back and pushed a pen into my hand. "Start your adventure, girlie."

I looked to Brady for confirmation that he'd meant it. He nodded. I had to clear my throat to speak again. "Um, sorry. Just to be clear, if I applied and got it, it could be on a temporary basis?"

There should have been a splashing sound effect on the soundtrack of my life at this moment. I'd decided to jump in.

But first I needed to check something. I faced Brady, pushing my suitcase to the side as I stepped closer to him. "How long until the hiring goes through?"

He scratched his head, looking up and squinting one eye like he was dragging up info from the cloud. "A week, maybe two. I'd have to ask HR. Why? You can meet us at the next port if you're hired."

I had another idea. "What if I cash in my prize

now? Take my two weeks on board and shadow Angela a little, see if it's the job for me?"

Edie clasped her hands and gave a little squeal. "Brilliant!"

Brady grinned. "Let's find out."

The four of us scuttled across the ship to the staff administration office where Brady disappeared into the maze of cubicles that reminded me of the maze I used to keep stocked with little cheese prizes for our classroom mouse Felix when I was a kid.

I told this to Edie who laughed. "You're not wrong. I used to work in one back at the resort. The only thing missing in one of these things is the cheese."

Kevin chimed in, "That is, unless Brady comes back with gouda news."

Edie and I went silent and looked at Kevin, who was cringing at his own joke with a crinkled nose and finger guns. We both burst out laughing, which had the folks working in the maze, er, cubicles, popping up to peer over their walls like startled meerkats.

"Sorry," Edie whispered. "We're waiting for Brown Eyes."

The meerkats sank back into the maze and Brady, aka Brown Eyes, returned with a solemn face.

My fingers that had been so tight and anxious holding my single suitcase loosened and it rolled away like I imagined my hopes doing. I guess it was back to humiliation at home for me after all.

Brady stopped my luggage escaping with a well-placed foot.

"It's okay," I started, ready to pretend I hadn't been hoping and praying, but Brady silenced my spiel by handing me a key card and an envelope. My heart did a little flip. "What's this? Is it--"

Brady nodded, his face all smiles now.

"You're registered. New room will be ready tonight. You're in luck. There was a last-minute cancellation and a stateroom down the hall from Edie and Kevin's became available." He reached out a hand to shake. "Welcome back aboard, Ms. Watson."

Edie whooped and Kevin patted me on the back awkwardly, his grin wide as he said, "That is gouda news!"

Brady looked confused, but he joined in the laughter as we exited the offices before slipping another piece of paper into my hands the moment my feet hit the deck.

"No time like the present. Whatta ya say?"

I looked at my friends.

Edie nodded. Kevin mimed signing with a flourish, and Brady handed me the pen from his shirt pocket.

With a shaking hand, I uncapped the pen and scrawled my info and my signature on the application before I could change my mind.

Brady took the paper from my hand, and Edie produced a bottle of champagne from her giant purse.

What had I done?

Edie whooped. "That's settled, and it's time to celebrate!"

She started passing out plastic champagne flutes, also somehow coming from her bottomless bag, motioning to Kevin as she did.

At her cue, Kevin raised his camera to Brady. "Grandma wants a picture of this moment."

I took the champagne she gave me, feeling light-headed without the bubbly. *Had I lost my mind? This was so not on my ten-year plan.*

I gave in and nodded at the champagne in Edie's hand. "You took a gamble, didn't you?"

Edie smiled, clinking her plastic glass to mine. "Oh, I never gamble, remember? I have a system."

"Yes, yes, you do." I drank to my own success, happy to be surrounded by new friends and a new opportunity. Things looked uncertain, sure, but I couldn't help feeling like I'd just spun the wheel and landed on double zero.

I had friends, I had two weeks cruising to parts unknown, since I hadn't bothered to check the destination of my impromptu cruise, and I had a shot at a new job.

I glanced up at Brady, whose gaze was fixed on my face. Maybe I had a shot at more than a new job.

But that was a ship I wasn't ready to sail. Maybe never again. For now, I'd just enjoy the warm look in his brown eyes and the friendships I had in my corner.

I took another drink of the celebratory champagne. For the second time on this trip, I realized maybe I was a winner.

THE END

About the Author

GWEN TAYLOR

I write cozies to give readers escape and adventure into a light-hearted, feel-good world. Because that's what I want! All I need to bliss out is a cozy, a cuppa, and my big fluffy doggo by my side. Well, that and fresh green beans and a big juicy tomato from my heirloom veggie garden!

I also write sweet, clean romance and romantic suspense. Most of my stories are set in Southern Appalachia to share the beauty and majesty and romance of the mountains I am grateful to call home.

Gwen Taylor lives in the woods near the Appalachian Trail where she is inspired by the view that is both beautiful and haunting. She belongs to a fluffy dog named Ralph and serves as his butler, opening and closing the door as many times per day as he wishes.

Subscribe HERE to get your free novella! And join my FB page HERE.

JEN BOOKER

I write cozy mysteries to entertain and escape into fun worlds. I like nothing better than curling up under a blanket with a hot cuppa and a good cozy mystery on a rainy English day! When I'm not reading or writing, I can usually be found knitting, crocheting, or walking in the English countryside.

Find her FB page HERE.

Jen Booker lives in England and spends her time writing feel-good stories and baby-sitting her granddog.

Also by Gwen Taylor

BY GWEN

/\

A DEADLY MEMORY

A LOVE TO REMEMBER

BY GWEN & JEN

/\

SINISTER SAILING: A MIA WATSON CRUISE SHIP
MYSTERY

DEADLY DINING: A MIA WATSON CRUISE SHIP
MYSTERY

FILM FATALE: A MIA WATSON CRUISE SHIP MYSTERY

Join our cozy crew! Gwen's & Jen's Cozies & Cuppas
Crew https://www.facebook.com/groups/
504967698485231